Beauty's Curse

a Love on the High Seas novel

Beauty's Curse

a Love on the High Seas novel

TAMARA HUGHES

Entangled Publishing, LLC
2614 South Timberline Road
Suite 109
Fort Collins, CO 80525
Visit our website at www.entangledpublishing.com.

Scandalous is an imprint of Entangled Publishing, LLC.

Edited by Erin Molta
Cover Design by Libby Murphy & Liz Pelletier
Cover Art by 123RF & iStock

ISBN 978-1-943336-36-4

Manufactured in the United States of America

First Edition June 2015

To Brenna and Megan. You inspire me in more ways than you know. Love you.

Chapter One

A crisis of her own making, yet again. Would she ever be free of this curse that followed her? Amelia's throat constricted with dread. She hung tight to the railing and looked out across the Atlantic at the approaching ship. Its red flag billowed in the breeze under a cloudless afternoon sky. Even if the captain hadn't pointed it out as a pirate ship, the flag displaying a skull with a dagger clenched between its teeth evinced the proof.

"We're to surrender?" the first mate, Ellis Rixon, asked.

As if they could do much else.

Captain Tuttlage's expression turned grim. "We have no other choice. Without their aid we're sure to die. We have but hours left before *Fortune's Song* sinks to the bottom of the sea."

All too true. Already the ship listed, and the decks slanted at an angle she could barely manage, although the crew had no such issue. Some even rested on the floor, exhausted from pumping water from the leaking hull these last three days. Most kept their sights on her, giving her a wide berth. They blamed her for this disaster. As well they should. If only she'd listened to her father's pleas. She had no business sailing across the ocean, not with her affliction.

"Look sharp," the captain ordered, and all hands rose to attention. "Proceed," he told his first mate.

Mr. Rixon grumbled, but held a white cloth high and waved it back and forth.

The pirate vessel closed in until it was nearly upon them, and from its decks a sound carried. A violin. She'd never heard such music before. The notes were strong and forceful, almost aggressive in nature. A song to urge men into battle.

Grappling hooks found their mooring, and soon a plank allowed passage between the two vessels. All manner of men waited on the far deck, heavily armed. Throughout the duration of settling the ships together, many stood watch with pistols and muskets at the ready.

Her legs shook beneath her petticoats and her hands grew clammy. She searched for anything that might bring her comfort. The violinist. She focused on him. He gripped his violin in a steady hand, the base clamped under his chin and the bow held loosely but with purpose. His face to the side, he paid no heed to the activity around him. If only she could do the same.

One man stepped forth, climbing onto the plank. She ignored him as best she could. Better to concentrate on something less frightening than let her fear get the best of her, or she might melt into a quivering mass right here on the deck. She studied the musician's relaxed stance, his lean jaw, the dark lashes that framed eyes she couldn't see…his mop of dark brown hair…

"Do you surrender?" the lone fellow on the plank asked.

"Aye. We do," Captain Tuttlage shouted back.

What would their surrender entail? After all, they'd be under the command of pirates. Her gaze turned to the violinist's fingers, slender and dexterous.

"Good to hear." The man on the plank waved his hand toward his ship. "I'm Captain Swain, and you're welcome to come aboard."

Welcome? Her attention darted to Captain Swain. Instead of a severe mien and an air of menace expected from a leader of pirates, he had a relaxed bearing that suggested mercy. Could it be true?

"Our thanks." Captain Tuttlage nodded to his men who looked amongst themselves before grudgingly moving forward. One by one they boarded the pirate ship until only she, the first mate, and Captain Tuttlage remained.

"We should leave her here," Mr. Rixon advised Captain Tuttlage. "She's caused us nothing but trouble."

Panic jolted through her, smashing what was left of her fortitude like shattering glass. Would they leave her behind to die? Her grip on the rail tightened, her shoulders so tense they ached. She shouldn't be surprised by Mr. Rixon's suggestion. Once their misadventures had begun, he'd been the first to herald her as the cause.

The captain shook his head. "I won't have it. In good conscience, I can't sentence her to death."

"But you see what she's done here," Mr. Rixon exclaimed, his arms swinging wide toward the deck of their sinking ship.

"Nonsense. Be off with you."

The first mate's icy blue stare bored into her before he stepped onto the plank.

"My lady." Captain Tuttlage extended his hand.

She glanced toward the pirate ship. What awaited her there? She'd been safe enough on *Fortune's Song*. Relatively safe, anyway. But pirates? From what she'd heard, they held no honor, no regard for life or limb.

With the captain's help, she climbed to the plank. He steadied her as she shuffled across, her eyes on her feet and her heart thumping hard. *I will not fall. The board will not break. The ocean will not swallow me up.*

An eternity passed by the time she reached the plank's end safely. She looked up, and her breath caught. All eyes were on her. Some stares held curiosity, some lust...others wariness—those faces she knew quite well. The crew of *Fortune's Song*, the ship she'd sunk.

The pirate captain cleared his throat and attention shifted to him. "Listen here. First matter to attend to... All those who have come from the sinking vessel, hand over your weapons."

Now that the crew of the merchantman had come aboard, many of the pirates had turned to swords and daggers for defense. Under their watchful eyes, the crew had little choice but to do as the pirate captain ordered. Soon a pile of firearms and blades lay on the deck at Captain Swain's feet.

"William," Captain Swain called out. "As you spotted our guests' sail first, you can choose the finest pistol of the lot."

A pirate with flaming red hair stepped forward, a wide grin on his face. "Aye, cap'n." He quickly picked up the gun Captain Tuttlage had relinquished.

"Now then, a question." Captain Swain addressed his

prisoners once more. "How have you fared under your captain and officers? Have they treated you well?"

An odd question. Even if they'd been mistreated, they wouldn't be sailing for those officers any longer. She glanced at Captain Tuttlage who stood with confidence, his head held high. From what she'd seen, the men under his command had always respected him and followed his orders with no complaint, as evidenced by their ready nods now.

Captain Swain smiled his acceptance. "As to the future, each of you who have just boarded *The Wanderer* will be given a choice. You can join up with us, or you can retire to the hold and be ransomed to your kin." He gestured to Captain Tuttlage with an apologetic look. "Obviously you'll be relegated to the hold as we have no need for another captain."

"What of the girl?" someone shouted. "Can she join the crew?"

A bout of laughter followed the remark until Mr. Rixon spoke up. "I say she be left behind."

Her pulse beat at a maddening pace, and she wrapped her arms around herself. If Mr. Rixon succeeded in swaying these men, she might drown yet this day.

· · ·

His violin and bow dangling at his sides, David studied the woman in question. He couldn't help himself. Demure in her simple blue gown, her hair pulled beneath a lace cap, she had a tiny build, fragile and delicate. Her blond hair as light as the sun, full pink lips, and an innocent face so youthful and radiant… He could scarce tear his attention away.

"Left behind?" Captain Swain shook his head. "For what cause?"

"She's bad luck. Ask any of our crew."

Judging by the full suit he wore, complete with surcoat, stockings, and a plumed tricorn, the one who spoke was the first mate of the captured ship.

The man looked about, and those who had come with him bobbed their heads. The first mate swept his arm toward the wreckage they'd come from. "She sank our ship and got us captured by pirates."

"Rubbish," the man's captain interjected.

"Silence," Captain Swain told him. "You, sir, are a prisoner now. This is for the crew, both new and old, to decide."

"There's more," the first mate insisted. "We barely survived a storm."

Shouts of agreement came from the first mate's crew, and the girl took a step back, her eyes wide. The fright on her face was more than he could take.

"You blame her for a storm?" David called out, gaining him curious looks from his own brethren, particularly William, who knew him best of any here.

The first mate wouldn't be outdone. "We've also suffered with fire, snapped ropes—"

"All common enough when at sea," David argued, his hand gripping his violin in a strangling hold. *Who was this man who would so easily sentence a woman to death?*

"What do you know of it?" The first mate scowled and stepped toward him. "You weren't there. I was."

Captain Swain turned to the girl, his expression merely curious. "What do you think, my lady? Are you the cause of these misfortunes?"

She scanned the men on deck, her breath coming in gasps.

A ridiculous question. "Do you expect her to answer?" David scoffed. If she said yes, they'd throw her overboard, and if no, they wouldn't believe her.

His own crew murmured around him. "A woman on board is bad luck. She'll be the end of us."

"What superstitious nonsense." David crossed the deck to stand before her and faced his fellow crewmen. "Don't listen to this man. He may have been first mate on the other ship, but he's no one here."

"I'm not speaking as first mate," the man growled and strode ahead. "I'm speaking as someone who'd rather not die because of the likes of her."

David handed his violin and bow to William, then drew his sword. "No one touches the girl."

William's red brows shot to his hair. David couldn't blame him. In the eight months David had sailed with this lot, he'd kept to himself, never drawing attention good or bad. But blaming a woman for random ill fortune, to threaten her life. He couldn't abide such injustice.

Although Captain Swain could have taken affront at David's dictate, he contemplated the situation with an amused smile. "You'd fight for her?"

His sword still held in front of him, he spared no thought before he answered. "Yes."

Captain Swain's smile broadened as he turned to the crew at large. "What say you? This could be most enjoyable." He nodded to the first mate. "You there. What's your name?"

"Ellis Rixon."

"Very good." Captain Swain spread his arms wide. "Do you wish to fight our David here for the right to decide the girl's fate?"

Rixon didn't hesitate. "I do." He shed his surcoat and hat, handing them to another.

"Well then," Captain Swain said. "If you win, she'll be returned to your sinking ship. If David is victorious, she'll remain on board under his protection."

Rixon picked up a sword from the pile on the deck. "Agreed."

"Lay aside those blades, lads. I won't risk a crewman for the sake of settling a disagreement," Captain Swain warned. "No weapons allowed. The one who draws first blood is the victor."

David set down his sword and watched as Rixon did the same. The captain's order came as no surprise. He'd heard the same before. In fact, he'd counted on it. He'd been trained at an early age to defend himself with fisticuffs. His father had seen to that. Bitterness welled up like poison in his belly. Making his sons prove themselves to be proper men had been important to his father.

He raised his fists and assumed a fighting stance. This might be the one time his father had been right in his thinking.

Rixon followed his lead, and they circled each other slowly as the crew cheered. David observed his opponent, how he moved and held his hands. The way his eyes darted from one location to the next suggested Rixon wasn't a patient man. He'd be the first to—Rixon lashed out. David jerked away, avoiding a blow to the face. Only a matter of seconds passed, and Rixon swung again. David dodged to the right, and Rixon once again met air.

"Do you plan to do nothing but prance about?" Rixon sneered. "Are you afraid to fight me?" Another swing. David ducked and struck out, connecting solidly with Rixon's jaw. Rixon staggered back, a look of shock on his face.

His brethren roared with satisfaction, and triumph surged through David's veins. Rixon. What an overconfident peacock. And yet the posturing harrier was the kind of man his father would have been proud to call son.

Rixon's gaping surprise soon changed to annoyance. He lunged, his fist thrusting forward. It met its mark, and pain blasted through David's jaw. His father had often called him weak. Too soft.

He received a blow to the ribs, knocking the air from his lungs. Despite the loud cheers and hoots, he heard a soft gasp from behind him. *Never good enough.*

Rage burned through him like a wick set ablaze. He punched Rixon in the eye, then his stomach. *Why can't you be more like your brother?* His brother James was a good man, the best. He was a sailor, a captain full of ambition... David landed a strike to Rixon's neck. The man clasped his throat and doubled over before something in his hand glinted in the sunlight. Rixon's arm made a wide arc, and the knife's edge traced a path across David's chest. The crowd jeered.

"See here. No weapons, I said." Captain Swain motioned to the two closest men, who quickly stepped forward, but Rixon took another swing at David, his blade out.

Enough. David knocked Rixon's arm to the side and seized his wrist. Giving it a hard wrench, David forced him to drop the knife, then bashed him in the nose with a solid hit. Rixon's blood trickled onto his white lace cravat as he dropped to his knees on the deck. He clutched his nose and glared with pure hatred.

One of the crewmen grasped Rixon by the back of his shirt and half dragged him to the captain, while the other fetched the fallen knife.

Captain Swain shook his head. "Ellis Rixon, for your treachery you forfeit your weapons," he chuckled, "your fancy clothes, and for a fortnight your rank is that of a cabin boy."

Rixon's lips thinned and his cheeks grew red at the crew's laughter that followed, but he said not a word. Perhaps Rixon was smarter than David had taken him for.

Wasting no more time, Captain Swain shoved the girl toward David and addressed the prisoners. "Now then, make your choice—join us or be ransomed."

A soft body collided with his, and he grasped her arms to steady her. She regained her footing, her gloved hand on his chest, before her blue-green eyes stared up at him with gratitude. "I don't know how to thank you." Her gazed dropped to where her hand lay, and she snatched it back as a pink glow suffused her lovely face.

He drank in the sight of her sweet innocence.

"Your chest." The pink took on a deeper hue. "You're injured."

David peered down at the rip in his shirt and the slight oozing of blood. A shallow wound. "Nothing to worry over. Merely a scratch."

"I should tend it," she insisted. "You were injured because of me."

He imagined her dainty hands touching him, bringing him ease, and pleasure licked down his spine. A part of him wanted to acquiesce and let her do what she would. Another warned him to stay clear, both for his protection and hers.

"No need. I'll heal soon enough." He turned toward Captain Swain.

"Ho, Captain," David called out as William handed him his violin and bow before joining the others across the plank to scavenge the sinking ship.

Swain regarded him with an eyebrow arched in question.

"Where will…" David leaned toward the girl at his side. "What's your name?"

"Miss Amelia Archer," she answered, the lyrical quality of her voice as attractive as the rest of her.

"Where will Miss Archer be staying until her family claims her?" he finished. In the hold with the men was out of the question, and as the ship's musician, he had no cabin to offer.

The captain rubbed his chin for the space of a minute, then nodded. "Procter will give up his cabin for the remainder of the voyage. See it done."

Procter uttered a curse. The carpenter and sometimes surgeon strode toward them, his balding head shining from the sun's rays. "I'll remove my things."

"My thanks," Amelia said as he passed by.

Procter ignored her. *Dammit.* Another crewman with a grievance against her. He'd best be on his guard and prepare himself, for this voyage might prove to be a long one.

Chapter Two

Amelia paced the cabin she'd been given. She should be asleep, but the thoughts churning in her head didn't allow her any peace. She didn't even go to the trouble of changing for bed. Despite Mr.... What was his surname? *Hmm*. Despite *David's* earlier heroics, how many of the crew still wanted her gone? A simple lock on a door wouldn't keep them at bay if they were determined to throw her overboard.

Her attention caught on the bowl of stew sitting on the small table. She cringed. The notion of food turned her stomach. Even if she managed to survive until they reached England, she didn't want to return. She'd left her home for a reason. To keep her father and her stepsister safe. To finally find a place to live out her days without worrying she'd cause more pain.

Melodic strains of a violin carried through the door. A soft, sleepy song. *David*. By the sounds of it, he played just outside her cabin. For several moments, she stood still, listening. The music calmed and soothed her frayed nerves as sure as a hand stroking her back.

When the song ended, she opened her door. David sat on a lone chair in the corridor. His dark brown hair was shaggy, as if he hadn't a care about his appearance. The notes he'd played lingered like the memory of a caress, and her gaze strayed to the deep V of his loose white shirt. It displayed a great deal of his sculpted chest, and his tan breeches... They molded over his thighs, emphasizing his lean muscular legs, and ended at his knees, his calves and feet bare.

Soulful brown eyes stared back at her, and she glimpsed a bruise along his jaw—another injury that could be laid at her feet. Under his regard, a tingling sensation flitted through her belly, and her nerves frayed for a whole different reason.

"Your music is lovely," she blurted. "Were you playing for me?" *Why did I ask that?* She'd never been so bold before.

He peered at her with a light in his eyes that gave her the answer she sought, and those tingles sprang to life once more. He glanced toward the ceiling. "Captain Swain's cabin is above us. Sometimes he requests that I play when he can't sleep."

"Not tonight?"

The corner of his lips twitched. "Not tonight." He set aside the violin and bow. "Although I don't play much at all anymore unless ordered."

"Why? Your music is extraordinary."

He ran his fingers along the strings. "I've lost the love of playing."

"That can't be. No one makes music as you do without emotion."

Curiosity wrinkled his brow. "What does it matter?"

She detected a sadness about him that belied his words.

It mattered a good deal. "You couldn't have become so proficient without much practice. At one time, your playing must have been a great passion."

"At one time."

What had happened to bring about such change? Especially in one so young. One who appeared to be not much older than herself. "I find it sad to think something that gave you pleasure has now become a burden."

He turned his attention to the floor. "Did I wake you?"

Very well. He wouldn't talk to her now, but possibly later. "No, I can't sleep."

"Why would that be?"

Why indeed, with Mr. Rixon against her. "Does your captain always invite those he captures to join his crew?"

He shook his head. "We lost many in our last battle, including our old captain. This one was only elected last month."

One month. Given his lack of experience leading the crew, would the captain's authority be respected, his orders followed? "Mr. Rixon won't relent in his crusade to have me removed from the ship, regardless of your captain's decision to allow me to stay." Lord knew he'd been an incessant burr in Captain Tuttlage's side. If Captain Tuttlage hadn't been so resolute in keeping her safe, Rixon might have already succeeded in casting her off.

"Why? Is he highly superstitious?"

"I suppose that would be one reason."

"Does he have others?"

She could tell him of Mr. Rixon's advances, but that had occurred months ago. He hadn't dared since, not after Captain Tuttlage threatened to toss *him* overboard if he didn't capitulate. No, a more likely answer came to mind. "It seems to me that Mr. Rixon likes to have everyone's ear."

"Yes, I see that he does." David scowled. "He's not on our decks but minutes before he's flapping his gums about nonsense. No doubt it's a ploy to raise his importance in the eyes of the crew. If he can somehow make them believe he speaks the truth, they'll come to rely on his advice more and more."

Dear God. How soon before he has me thrown from the ship? Her worry must have shown.

David dropped his hand to the hilt of the sword at his waist, and his eyes darted to hers. "I promise I'll do my best to protect you."

Something in her chest squeezed tight. Was that why he sat outside her door? Of course. But their journey would be a long one. He couldn't stand guard night and day. He'd need to rest sometime. "You can't stay out here all night."

"I can and I will."

"What about sleep?"

"I can't afford to sleep." His head cocked to the side as if he didn't understand why she'd question him. "You have the right of it. Rixon isn't the type to give up because of one defeat. In fact, he'll likely be more determined than ever to convince everyone of their plight. And the crew, they're a superstitious lot."

Warmth spread through her. This man would defend her to the last. "At least come inside. You can sleep knowing you'll have time to react if someone attempts to break through the door."

His dark gaze slid down her body and back up, hesitating briefly at her square bodice. "I shouldn't."

Her breath caught at his perusal. He was right. It would

be improper, but for the best of intentions. "I trust you." After all, he was the sole reason she still lived.

David swallowed hard. "Perhaps you're too trusting."

So she'd been told repeatedly by her father, but this time she was sure. "Please," she insisted. "I'll feel safer knowing you're there." No man could live without sleep. What if he nodded off and was taken by surprise?

Pinching the bridge of his nose, he released a long exhale. "If that's what you wish." He retrieved his instrument from the floor and extinguished his lantern.

She led the way. Although the cabin's size prevented her from going far, she moved to stand before the small table by the bed. "Where would you like to—"

He strode through the door, his head nearly brushing the top of the frame. He was taller than he'd seemed in the corridor, and bigger, more virile.

She gave him the key. He secured the lock and handed it back, then sat down on the planks in front of the door. "Here will do."

The tingling had become much stronger now. "Good." Clumsily, she half turned toward the bedside table, her feet tangling. She grasped the table behind her for support and attempted to act as if the misstep had never occurred. "Would you like the light?"

An amused smile raised one side of his mouth, not that she could blame him. "You can extinguish it and settle in bed," he replied.

In bed…with a man in her room. "Yes, of course." She straightened and spun about, bending to blow out the candle.

"Wait!" David's arm snatched her around the waist, and he lifted the back of her petticoat.

"What are you…" She tried to twist away, but he held her in place and pounded her behind with her gown! *Dear Lord. What madness is this?*

He let out a rush of air, and his arms slackened around her, her hem returning to the floor. "You were on fire."

"I was?" She looked behind and spied the slightest bit of charred lace.

David peered over her shoulder. "A candle… You're never to carry a candle without a lantern aboard ship. The punishment is Moses's Law."

"I wasn't carrying it." She stepped away, his hands on her person unnerving. Yet as soon as they were gone, she wished them back. How long had it been since she'd felt the comfort of a touch? She pushed aside the unwelcome thought. "What is Moses's Law?"

He blew out the candle. "It's forty lashes less one on the bare back." His voice, a low rumble in the dark, released a flutter of moths in her belly.

She cleared her throat. "Why less one?"

"I'm not sure," he answered.

The window provided almost no light from the waning moon. Only the barest shadow moved when David stepped back to the door. Back to the door. Good. She'd best not become too attached to him. Friends, family, any person who became close to her suffered. Her heart couldn't take another such blow.

"Some say it's biblical, that thirty-nine lashes is one less than a death sentence."

She brushed at the back of her dress, wondering how much damage had been done. "And others?"

"Others say the Romans demanded that their floggers

kill a man within forty lashes, and if they didn't, they would be put to death."

"Then punishment for carrying a candle without a lantern is not death, just close to death."

"Yes."

"A pleasant story." She climbed into bed and lay down. "No need to go on."

A chuckle reached her from his side of the room, bringing a smile to her face. From the first moment they'd met, David had seemed too serious by far. How good to hear him laugh. Several minutes passed as she lay wide awake. With David so close, the dark bedeviled her. The silence even worse. "You fought well today," she finally said, but frowned as guilt soured her stomach. Would he have gone to the trouble if he knew what Mr. Rixon had said was true? He hesitated so long, she wondered if he'd already fallen asleep, or could read minds.

"I've been trained to use my fists, but today was the first time I've had to put my skills to good use."

Ah, she'd pushed him into his first fistfight. That knowledge did little to ease her guilt. Then again, he was a pirate. No doubt he'd helped his crew capture ships, and he did have a sword on his belt. He may not have fought with fists before, but he most assuredly had used his blade. Somehow that didn't make her feel any better. She'd still been the reason he'd argued against members of his own crew, and became her protector.

"What's your surname?" she asked. The least she could do was address him properly.

"Lamont."

"Thank you again for what you did for me today, Mr. Lamont." She sincerely hoped she hadn't put him in further danger.

"I'd prefer it if you called me David."

"Very well…David." After all he'd done, she would allow the same. "You may call me Amelia."

A soft laugh rode his breath. "My apologies, but I intended to all along."

• • •

David accompanied Amelia to the deck, staying close to her side. "You'd be safer in the cabin."

She raised her face skyward, her cheeks flushed and her eyes bright. "Then I'd miss this sunshine." Closing her eyes, she basked in the rays before opening one lid and casting him a sideways glance. "Besides, I've been thinking." She strolled over to the rail and gazed out at the sea. "Your captain must have some say over the crew if they elected him. No one would dare harm me without his permission, unless they're willing to pay his price, and I suspect the consequences for disobeying him would be significant."

Amelia was right on all counts, except one. "Unless the perpetrator could do the deed without getting caught."

The spark in her eyes dimmed, and he cursed himself for planting the worry she now carried. Curse it. Her safety was his responsibility. If he did his job well, she shouldn't have to concern herself. "Don't listen to me," he assured her. "The deck is nearly empty, and even if it wasn't, no one would be so bold as to threaten you in plain view."

Amelia's shoulders relaxed. "I'm sure you're right."

As she stared out over the horizon, David scanned the deck. Strange. Why were there so few at their posts? What was meant to reassure Amelia now prickled the hairs on the nape of his neck. All those missing could be congregating, planning a way around the captain's order, or arguing with Captain Swain to change his mind. Rixon had been so emphatic that she be left behind, he most likely wouldn't let the matter rest. Still, no mishaps had happened thus far, other than the candle, but no one knew about that. The crew may be superstitious, but their fears would fade with time. And the captain… He wouldn't alter his decision without good reason, not if he wanted to be looked upon as a decisive leader.

No, something else wasn't right. He lifted his sights to the blue sky and the slack sails. Slack? His attention had been on Amelia or he might have noticed before. The air was still and stagnant. No wind at all, not even the slightest breeze. Unusual but not unheard of. It also explained the empty deck. The crew could relax with the ship becalmed.

A movement caught his eye.

William stepped from the shadows and headed toward them, his usual smile in place and Rixon's tricorn on his head—the white plume identifying its rightful owner. "A beauty of a day, is it not?"

"Indeed," David replied. "Amelia, may I introduce William? William, this is Amelia."

"A pleasure it is, dear lass." A dimple appeared in William's freckled cheek as his smile broadened.

"I see you have a new hat," David pointed out, "courtesy of our cabin boy."

William turned his head side to side. "Aye. Do you like it?"

"Aye, I do." David gave Amelia a wink. Perhaps they

wouldn't have to worry overmuch about Rixon.

"What has happened to Mr. Rixon?" she asked.

Was that concern he detected on her face? Why?

"Never fear, lass. Rixon is quite well, just busy," William said. "Been emptyin' the piss tubs and takin' orders from whoever might give them. It's been grand fun."

David's soft laugh joined William's. Rixon's pride might never recover.

"What of his predictions of tragedy and death?"

"Ah, they never end," William confirmed. "It seems Amelia here has caused our lack of wind, she has."

Sadness crept over Amelia's features. *Damn Rixon and his stories.*

William lifted his hands. "No worries. The crew is payin' him no heed, not with a celebration upon us."

"Celebration?" Amelia asked.

"This afternoon we'll be celebratin' our latest conquest," William nodded to David, "with *music*, games, and drinkin'. All are expected to come and enjoy." He peered at Amelia. "Includin' you."

"I-I don't know…" she stuttered.

"Of course she'll come," David answered for her. He couldn't adequately watch over her in the cabin if he'd be required to play for the men on deck.

Amelia didn't argue. In fact, her face lit up as if well pleased by the news.

"Well, I'd best get below," William said, a smile fighting to reappear. "About now is my turn again to make a request of our cabin boy." His smile did break through then. "Maybe I'll have him rockin' me hammock while I take a nap. After all, I need to be well rested for the comin' festivities." His steps lively, he returned to the door leading below deck and disappeared.

"A party," Amelia sighed. "It's been so long since I've been to one."

"This won't be an elegant social event," he reminded her. "These are pirates who will drink to excess, sing bawdy tunes, and swear until your ears burn."

She ignored his warning, the pleased expression still on her face. "William seems like a nice fellow."

"He is," David agreed, remembering how the man had annoyed him at first. At the time, William's jovial disposition had grated. That and his persistence.

"William is the type of man who must be friends with everyone, even with those who have no interest in being friends with him."

"Why is that?"

He'd asked himself that same question countless times. "I don't know, but it drives him mad if he thinks someone doesn't like him. He'll do everything in his power to change that person's mind." At least that's how William had been with him. "No doubt it has something to do with how happy he is to be on this ship. This is his home now."

She turned back toward the calm ocean waters, her gloved hands on the rail. "What did he do before?"

"He served aboard a Royal Navy ship, but not by choice." William had told him the whole story. "He'd been drinking in a London tavern not far from the docks, and when he reached the bottom of his cup, he found a shilling had been dropped into his ale."

"A shilling?"

"Aye. By the Navy's way of thinking, it's an advance

payment for joining up."

"Through trickery," she scoffed.

"Doesn't matter. They forced him aboard and locked him below decks whenever they reached port so he couldn't escape."

One eyebrow quirked. "Does that have anything to do with why Captain Swain asked the crew of *Fortune's Song* if their officers had treated them well?"

"It does. As sailors, it's our duty to ensure others of our like are treated fairly."

She cast him a glance rife with suspicion. "If they're not?"

"The officers would be punished."

"In what way?" She brushed her hand over the rail, tracing the grain of the wood, avoiding his gaze as if preparing herself for the worst.

"That depends on what was done to the crew." Typically offending officers were whipped or shot, but no sense unsettling her with those details.

"In the case of William's superiors?" She flinched and inhaled a sharp gasp, flipping her hand over to peer down at her palm and a small rip in her glove.

He'd best not say. Instead he posed the question that had troubled him since he first spied Amelia. "Why were you traveling alone?"

"I wasn't. Not at first." A flash of pain crossed her face that had nothing to do with the sliver she revealed when she tugged off her glove. "I'm going to live with my aunt in Virginia, and I had a maid who wanted to come with me."

"Only a maid? Two women amongst a ship of men?" He smothered a curse. "Where is this maid?" he asked, although he suspected he already knew.

She blinked away the wetness in her eyes and attempted to pick the sliver from her skin. "She took sick shortly after we set sail, and never recovered."

"I'm sorry."

Her blue-green eyes met his with a mixture of sadness and trepidation. "What if…" She stopped and took a breath. "What if what the crew says about me is fact?" she asked.

"I don't believe in superstition. Do you?"

No answer. She stared down at the splinter still lodged in her palm.

He pulled his dagger from its sheath and grasped her injured hand in his. "You believe you're bad luck?" *How did she get such a notion in her head?*

She sniffled, tears glistening in her eyes. "Bad things happen most everywhere I go."

Her misery gripped his heart and held firm. "Nonsense. Bad things happen to everyone. It's part of life." His assurance had no effect. She looked as unhappy as before. "You know windless days are fairly common." He used the knife's blade to free the sliver.

Amelia nodded and sniffed once more.

He resheathed his blade and bent forward to catch her eye. "It has nothing to do with you. Neither does a ship sinking."

"Why are you helping me? Your crew will come to see it as a betrayal."

"So be it." Save William's friendship, he'd never felt a part of the crew, anyway. "I have two older sisters. Between them and my mother, rest her soul, they taught me to respect women, cherish them…" he brushed his finger over a tendril of blond hair that dangled along her face, "protect them. And that's what I aim to do."

Chapter Three

In the shade of a listless sail, Amelia sat on a crate next to David as he played his violin. The pirates were dressed much the same as the crew of *Fortune's Song*, in rude, sailcloth breeches and simple loose shirts, with gold earrings dangling from their ears—used to pay for a proper grave should they die at sea. Die at sea. Sadly, over the course of her journey, some had. If only she could be sure they hadn't perished because of her presence. Hadn't David insisted that fires and accidents weren't all that uncommon?

Thankfully, thus far, all had been safe aboard *The Wanderer*. The pirate crew lounged on deck beneath the afternoon sun, playing dice and singing songs. David began the melody of *Greensleeves*, and several men raised their cups and sang along. "Greensleeves was all my joy. Greensleeves was my delight..."

Some voices held the notes, others... She suppressed a laugh at the robust, discordant attempts. Such happy faces.

She loved the chatter, the chuckles, the music. Safe at David's side, she tapped her foot in time to the rhythm.

A smooth baritone voice came nearer. "Greensleeves was my heart of gold." *William.* A cup in his hand, he strolled toward them. "Good day to you both."

David gave a nod and kept playing.

"Are you well rested?" she asked, her gaze darting to Mr. Rixon as he came through a door, bearing a platter of food.

William's smile answered her far quicker than words. "I am." He sipped from his cup, then fixed her with a curious stare. "Would you like to walk about? Maybe quench your thirst with a drink?"

"It might be best if she stayed with me," David spoke up before she could reply.

"All day?" William asked. "Sounds tiresome."

With a pleading look, she appealed to David's mercy. She'd sat on this crate for the better part of two hours. A walk would be refreshing.

"I'll keep her safe," William promised. "Have no worry of that. Don't you trust me?"

"Of course I do," David said. "But—"

"Then it's settled." William held out his arm. "Let's be off."

Eager to leave her perch, she stood and took his arm. "I won't be gone long," she told David. The concern in his eyes touched her deeply, but they wouldn't go far. He needn't worry.

She and William roamed at a leisurely pace, but her thoughts hadn't moved from David's side. "What do you know of David?"

"Not as much as you might expect." William glanced

back at the man in question. "He's not one to talk, especially about anythin' of a personal nature."

"How did he come to this ship? Were you on board at the time?"

"Aye, I was." He cringed and glanced at David again. "He boarded our ship in Madagascar, and a sorry-looking sight he was, too. Sunburned to the point of blisters, he wore only a waistcloth to cover his nakedness. And his eyes…" William frowned as if the memory disturbed him. "They were wild, like he'd seen or done something that would haunt his days his whole life long."

This time it was her turn to look at David. So strong and capable. She could hardly imagine him as the man William described.

"All he had with him was the violin he now plays, and that was plenty," William said. "We pirates value musicians like gold. Without them, we'd slash each other's throats to relieve the boredom."

Indeed? "You don't strike me as someone who would resort to violence as a form of sport."

"No," he agreed, a playful smile warming his face. "But not everyone aboard is as amiable as me."

She smiled back at him, the flirt. "I have no doubt that's true."

"A drink?" he asked, when they reached a barrel and pitchers that smelled of liquor. "Let's see…" he peeked inside a pitcher, "we've kill-devil…" He laughed at her confused look. "Better known as rum," he clarified as he glanced inside another container. "Ah, the crew's favorite— rum mixed with gunpowder."

Amelia wrinkled her nose. How could they drink such

a thing?

He peered into the last. "Ah, the captain's choice—bombo." William leaned closer. "That one I think you'll like. It's rum, water, sugar, and nutmeg."

He was right. Of the three, the third choice would suit her best. "Perhaps later."

They wandered amongst the men, some feasting on salted fish, cheese, and boiled potatoes, others gathered around a table to play a game of dice. She received a few wary looks, particularly from those newly made pirates from *Fortune's Song*.

"Lass," someone called from the table.

William at her side, she drew closer.

The man who'd called her was getting on in years. His silver hair scarce on the top of his head, he greeted her with a wide, nearly toothless smile. "I'm having the damnedest time getting good rolls of the dice," he said, his words slightly slurred. He waved her closer, and when she obliged, he wiggled his finger to draw her nearer still.

"How about a kiss for luck?" he said, loud enough for all to hear, before he let out a hearty whoop of laughter, his shoulders shaking and his face turning red.

The men around them howled along with him. Their gaiety infectious, soon she found herself laughing, too.

"Carry on all you want," Mr. Rixon's voice broke in. "You won't find luck with her." He carried a pitcher and refilled everyone's cups.

"Quit your blether," someone called out. "We've heard enough of your stories to last a lifetime."

"So you say now, but you'll soon come to my way of thinking," Mr. Rixon insisted. "Women don't belong on ships."

"What of Mary Read?" another asked. "She was a pirate."

"Married to Calico Jack Rackham," someone at the table added.

"Aye," Mr. Rixon agreed. "And we all know what happened to him and his. Captured and hung, put on display in a gibbet as a warning to us all."

Silence followed, and she clasped her hands together. She scanned the crew's faces, each pondering what Mr. Rixon had said. So absorbed by their reaction, she hadn't noticed that the music had stopped until David stood at her side.

"Enough of this," he said. "Has anything happened since she's been aboard?"

Several heads shook.

"He's right." William held his cup high. "Will we let Rixon ruin this day of celebration with his foolery? I say nay. Let's drink and enjoy!"

A cheer arose and cups were lifted. The revelry resumed as if Rixon had never spoken, but Amelia couldn't shake the dread that had her rubbing the raised bumps on her arms.

David settled his hand on the small of her back. "Come sit with me again."

She searched the crowd until her gaze came upon Captain Swain at the rail. "No, I'd like to make a request of the captain." She headed in his direction.

David strode beside her. "What request?"

Captain Swain watched as she approached. "What's your trouble?"

"Captain, would you mind if I delivered food and drink to the prisoners below?" She'd been meaning to visit Captain Tuttlage, and now seemed like a good time. Anything was

Beauty's Curse

better than staying on deck, at least until her nerves settled a bit. When the crew had been silent, as if contemplating her fate… She shivered.

"I wager the captain and crew of *Fortune's Song* won't want to celebrate their capture," Captain Swain said with a smirk.

"I think they'd appreciate food and drink no matter the reason." Lord knew how their prisoners were treated. She could only imagine.

"As you wish," the captain replied.

"No need to worry. They're well cared for," David told her.

She wouldn't be swayed in this. "I'd like to see for myself."

David rested a protective arm about her shoulders. "I'll go with her," he informed the captain.

Captain Swain shrugged. "If you must."

David showed her the way to the galley, where they gathered food and rum. They carried platters and pitchers down to the hold of the ship. To her surprise, laughter and merriment reached them before they descended the stairs. Well-placed lanterns lit the large space, and while the prisoners were shackled, they looked no worse for wear. Dishes of food, the same as above, circulated among them, and each had their own cup to drink from.

She cast a questioning look toward David.

"I told you they were well cared for," he said. "Each of these men will be ransomed. We'd best keep them healthy."

Not only kept healthy, they appeared in good spirits, too. She set down her platter in place of one already emptied and began refilling cups. When she came to Captain Tuttlage, she shook her head. "I'm so happy to see smiles down here.

I would have never thought…"

"Yes, I'm thankful we've been treated so well. I've heard tales of the horrors pirates can subject on their captives." The captain lifted his arm and the chain that dangled from it rattled. "Other than these shackles, I can't complain." Concern flooded his eyes. "What of you? Are you well?"

A reassuring smile rose into place. "Don't worry about me. I have my own cabin, and a guard." She peered over at David as he poured rum into waiting cups and spoke to the crew. "I'm in capable hands." At least for the moment. Given Mr. Rixon's comments on the deck and the reaction they elicited, she couldn't help but wonder how long she'd be safe.

• • •

The sun had set hours ago with the celebration unabated. As ordered, David played various jigs, his gaze straying to Amelia time and time again. William ever by her side, she'd joined the dancing, the light in her eyes and the sheer joy on her face captivating.

Given all the rum that had been consumed, the dancers were less than graceful. Even Amelia stumbled a time or two. Had she been drinking? He'd seen her with a cup in her hand but assumed it contained water. No matter. They'd be going back to her cabin soon. Over the course of the day, he'd watched the looks cast at Amelia change from curious or distrustful, to polite or downright friendly. In response, seemingly shy Amelia had blossomed before his eyes, interacting with the men with humor and grace. Beautiful beyond compare.

Of course, that had been some time ago, before the rum had taken hold. Now the glazed eyes of the men worried him. He would have swept her off to her cabin already if she didn't look so blessedly happy dancing amongst them. Had he ever been that happy, listening to music and enjoying the company of others? Perhaps a lifetime ago.

Yes, he'd give her more time. He'd play another song, maybe two, before he insisted she retire for the night.

He picked up his pace as he began a new jig, his fingers pressing the violin's strings in rapid succession and his bow gliding rhythmically. Amelia giggled, and he peered her way in time to see William twirl her about. She stumbled, her hand breaking away from William's, and bumped into someone's back, strong enough to send him tripping forward. He collided with two more, one of whom fell to the deck, knocking his nose on the hard planks. The pirate came up cursing and swinging, blood dripping from both nostrils. Landing a solid punch to one crewman and another, the injured man didn't stop fighting, and soon a good number of men had joined in the fray.

Bloody hell. David dropped his violin and bow, and charged in. Amelia had become separated from William. She stood in the midst of men who blindly struck out at anyone handy. As David shoved bodies out of his way, Amelia ducked and tried to escape the melee with no success. He finally reached her as a fist flew toward them. He wrapped an arm about Amelia's waist and hauled her out of harm's way, but didn't have time to do much more. Knuckles connected with his cheek, knocking his head to the side. Pain radiated along his face, and a coppery flavor sprang from a gash in his mouth.

He ignored it, his only thought to get her to safety. Amelia held close against him, he shouldered his way through the throng. Once free from the brawl, he retrieved his violin and took her hand as a shot rang through the air. Amelia jumped.

"Listen here, lads," Captain Swain called out. "Now that you've drunk your fill, be off to your beds. When the winds blow tomorrow, there'll be work to be done."

The men grumbled and cursed but obeyed their captain, each heading to his preferred sleeping place.

David tucked his violin beneath his arm and lifted his lantern, then tugged on Amelia's hand. "Let's get you to your cabin." He led the way, her hand never leaving his.

She stumbled behind him. "David, I'm sorry."

"You have no reason to be," he assured her.

"But I do. The fight began because of me."

He reached her door and ushered her inside. "If it hadn't been you, something else would have set them off. They're all drunk, and beating each other isn't as uncommon as you might think." David locked the door and pocketed the key. "You had a good time?"

Amelia sank down on the bed with a contented sigh. "I did. I had a lovely time."

"I'm glad."

She patted the spot next to her. "Come sit with me."

He shouldn't, but her eyes so bright, their color more green than blue in the lantern's glow, drew him to her. He sat, and her pleased smile intoxicated him more than rum ever could.

Amelia lifted her hand and brushed aside the hair on his forehead before teasing the strands at the nape of his neck. "Someone needs to trim your hair."

"Is that so?" he asked as he luxuriated in her touch. "Are

you that someone?"

"I could be."

Her finger skimmed along his throat to play with the opening of his shirt, and his pulse sped. What was this? When that same finger delved into his shirt front, her intention became obvious.

He stared deeply into her eyes. "Are you drunk?"

Amelia chuckled, a throaty sound that beckoned. "I don't know. Can one become drunk on one...no, two cups of..." She crinkled her nose as she concentrated.

For someone so small, it wouldn't take much. "What did you drink?"

She squeezed one eye shut as if it helped her to think. "The first cup was...bombo."

"The second?"

She smiled. "Frederick had a special wine he shared with me. He was really very kind. They all were."

Frederick. David almost groaned. "What kind of wine?"

"He called it wormwood." Her nose wrinkled again. "Quite bitter."

Damn Frederick.

Her palm cupped his cheek. "Now I'm pleasantly warm, and I feel like everything is so clear."

He had no idea what all went into Frederick's wine other than wormwood leaves, but that was enough to know the concoction was potent.

"You are a good man, David." Her thumb grazed over his lower lip, and she shifted a bit closer.

If she knew him better, she wouldn't say such a thing. Who he was, what he'd done... "You don't know what you're saying." He took her hand, placed it on her lap, and made a move to rise. "You should go to sleep."

"No, wait." She grasped his hand and pulled him back down. "Thank you for protecting me. Without you, I don't know what I would do." Leaning forward, she settled a quick kiss on his lips. Although the touch was fleeting, her soft mouth, flavored with the slightest hint of rum, tantalized his senses. His body's response was immediate and strong. He ached to hold her close and more thoroughly taste her lips. Through sheer will, he ignored the compulsion and moved to his uncomfortable bed in front of the door.

He blew out the lantern and struggled to sleep, his body and mind focused on the woman so close by, the feel of her slight kiss haunting him all night long.

Chapter Four

Amelia's head throbbed, although the ache was better than it had been when she first awoke. She followed David to the dining area on the ship. Like the prior day, the sails hung motionless and the deck was empty, save for a few sleeping crewmen.

When they reached the mess, it too was empty, although the time was almost noon.

"Strange," David said. "Even after their worst drunken nights, most still show up for a meal." He waved her ahead. "We'll head to the galley."

They traveled the short distance in a matter of minutes. An elderly man lay on a cot in the far corner of the small kitchen.

"George?" David approached him. "What goes?"

George wrapped his arms around his middle and groaned. "We're all sick."

"All?"

"Aye, nearly all. There were no space for me in the sick

room, so I had to come back here."

"What the devil?" David turned about and headed for the door at a quick pace.

Amelia trailed behind, her stomach plunging. *Please, Lord, no.*

It didn't take long to reach the sick room. Cots filled the space from wall to wall, and on each one lay a sailor in obvious distress. All the blood drained from her face.

"There she is," someone shouted. "The cause of all this."

She flinched. She knew that voice. Her gaze darted to Mr. Rixon, who occupied a cot like the rest, a greenish cast to his skin.

"Don't listen to him." David's arm came around her back as he moved to where William lay. "How do you fare?" he asked.

"How does it look?" William grumbled. "I'm dyin'."

Dying? Sweet Mary she hoped not.

David shook his head, a look of skepticism on his face. "I doubt that very much."

"We're all dying," Mr. Rixon moaned, "because of her."

A few scattered "Ayes" peppered the room, and she resisted the urge to cringe.

David's head snapped up. "Look here. She had nothing to do with this," he declared. "It's more likely your choice of mixing gunpowder with your rum made you sick."

"Not so," someone scoffed. "We been drinking our rum with powder for years with no trouble."

It was true. It had to be. They were all ill because of her. Her pulse stuttered a beat. A hand grasped hers. She looked down at William's warm green eyes.

"I don't blame you, lass," he said.

His confession tightened her chest all the more. He *should* blame her. She'd apologize here and now, but that would make matters worse. Instead, she squeezed his hand. William had been so kind to her, like David, like Captain Tuttlage. Oh no, Captain Tuttlage.

"If not the drink, then it's likely something you ate," David insisted.

"Are the prisoners ill?" she asked Procter. As the only one standing, he was obviously the *doctor* here, although he too looked a bit ashen.

Procter leaned against the wall and wiped the sweat from his brow. "No. They look well enough."

She released a breath. At least *they'd* been spared.

"See there," Mr. Rixon tried to push himself up but lay down with a grunt, "Captain Tuttlage, the one who defended her on *Fortune's Song*, isn't sick. Maybe she's a witch, ready to smite those who stand in her way."

A witch. If only she *could* control the curse that followed her.

"Gibberish," David called back. "Your illness has gone to your head."

"What of Frederick?" Mr. Rixon volleyed, pointing to a man asleep on a bed near the far wall, splints on both legs. "How do you explain his fall from the ratlines last night while on watch? Broke his legs."

Frederick? He'd been the one to give her his wormwood wine.

David scowled. "He, like the rest of you, was drunk. He had no business on the ratlines in that state."

"Can you explain away the wind?" This question came from another sailor, one she'd danced with last eve. "Still no breeze to fill our sails."

As the questions mounted, an awful warning niggled. How long before these men decided they'd had enough? And what would they do to her then?

"In this case, you should be thankful the sails are slack or you'd be working whether sick or not." David grasped her hand and took a step back as more voices joined in to grumble and blame.

"You'd best go," Procter advised. "Once their stomachs have settled, they'll be more likely to listen."

Would they? She sincerely hoped Procter was right.

"Rest well," David told William before he led her away. Outside the room, he continued toward the galley. "Pay no heed to that drivel."

"How can I not when it's likely true?"

He released a long sigh. "You can't mean that."

But she did, and it must have shown on her face because he stopped. Taking her by the arms, he stared into her eyes. "I don't understand how you can possibly accept that you're the cause of any of this."

"You've known me a couple of days. I've experienced events like this my whole life."

The doubt in his eyes still lingered. How could she explain? Maybe...

"When I was younger, I loved exploring the woods around our home. One day I reached the edge of the forest and came upon several men working in a field." She remembered it so vividly, the golden color of the wheat under the cloudless sky, the men swinging their scythes. "The sky was a perfect blue, but when I arrived, a lightning bolt struck the worker closest to me, killing him." She had known then, just as she knew now, that she was the cause. What else could it have been? That day, she'd run from that place as if the very devil were on her trail, and she'd never gone back.

"You may think you're somehow cursed, but I don't." He released her and ushered her ahead. "Regardless, you should keep your suspicions to yourself."

"I realize that." She'd rather not be thrown overboard.

"Now let's get lunch from the galley and return to the cabin. Last night you said you would trim my hair, and I'm going to hold you to it."

Her appetite was long gone. Whether David believed in her affliction or not didn't change the fact that it existed, and some day it would catch up with her.

• • •

David sat in a chair as Amelia snipped away at his overgrown mop of hair. He had to admit, he hadn't cut it since he'd left London... No. Had it been that long? He couldn't say. He'd all but given up caring what he looked like.

As she worked, her fingers trembled slightly and her face grew pinched, as if she worried she'd cut off his ear by mistake. The thought that this one small woman could bring misfortune to all around her was beyond absurd. "Does your family believe you're bad luck?"

Her hands stilled. "No. Not all of them."

Those words carried with them a weight of sadness he could almost feel. "I don't understand."

"My father and stepsister have always insisted it's superstition," she explained, "but my stepmother..." She worried her lip, her gaze fixed on his hair.

"Your stepmother told you that you're bad luck?"

Amelia frowned as she snipped away once more. "That and I have poor judgment."

"Why do you listen to her?" Her stepmother must be mad.

"I can hardly claim otherwise when the evidence is all around me. This curse has plagued me for years."

He should have guessed that would be her answer. "Is that why no family accompanied you on *Fortune's Song*? She convinced your father that traveling with you would be dangerous?"

"Not just her. I helped convince them." Amelia's spine straightened. "I vowed that I would go alone…though not completely alone…with my maid."

"To keep your family safe," he supplied, turning in his seat to look up at her face.

She inclined her head in agreement. Of all the silly, non-sensical… "What of your maid? Was she not worthy of the same protection?"

Amelia's features crumpled, and he cursed himself for reminding her of her maid's fate.

"I tried to dissuade her." Amelia's fingers combed through his hair with unnecessary roughness, checking its length. "She persisted, and my father gave his full support."

And after her maid's death, she had been alone, with only Captain Tuttlage to protect her. Anything could have happened. "Why now? You're a grown woman. If, as you said, you've carried bad luck your whole life, what changed that you would leave your family?"

She clutched the scissors in a tight grip. "There was an incident… I invited a beggar to stay in our home."

David looked at her askance. Had he heard her correctly?

"Just for the night," she quickly amended.

"And?"

"By morning he'd taken what valuables he could carry and disappeared. My stepmother declared that it was time for me to leave. She said my aunt's settlers' life would teach me hardship, make me less likely to allow others to take advantage," she muttered with a shake of her head. "He'd seemed so destitute, in need."

"Of course he did," he scoffed. "You're too trusting, by far. You should question what people want, understand their motives, before you give them such leeway." Which made him wonder… "What do you honestly think of Rixon and the crew blaming you for their troubles?"

She studied the scissors in her hand for a full minute before she spoke. "If I lived at sea and was always at the mercy of the elements, I'd likely do the same."

"You're excusing them?"

Her shoulders rose in a shrug. "We all like to have a reason behind the things that happen to us, to make us feel safer, less defenseless against fate."

"Ah, Amelia, what will I do with you?" he asked, sitting back in the chair. "You have a good heart… Much better than mine." At one time, he might have been as forgiving, but those days had long passed.

"I don't believe that. You're a good man, David." She slid her fingers through the hair on the back of his head, more gently this time, and he released a breath, savoring the light caresses. His mother had cut his hair when he'd been young, and his sisters had taken over the job after his mother had passed. He'd almost forgotten how much the simple act of

having his hair trimmed reminded him of home and family—
some memories good, and some better left forgotten.

"You mentioned going to live with your aunt in Virginia,"
he recalled.

"That's right."

"Do you know her well?"

"Only through letters." She measured a lock of hair
with her fingers and snipped off the ends. "She's lived in
the colonies for a long time now. To my father's dismay,
she married for love to a man who barely had a pence to
his name. Together they traveled to Virginia as indentured
servants and, once their debt was paid, took up farming."

"Sounds like a hard life."

"I'm sure it was, and still is, but Aunt Rosamond strikes
me as a tireless, sensible person who is capable of most
anything she puts her mind to." Amelia came around to his
side, taking care with every cut she made. "I started writing
her a few years ago after I'd heard her husband had passed…
I thought perhaps she was lonely."

Like Amelia? She hadn't said so, but he sensed her melan-
choly nevertheless. "Was she?" he asked.

"I could hardly tell. It seems she doesn't have the time to
think about such things."

David glanced over at Amelia. Such a tiny frame for
farm work. "Do you look forward to living with this aunt?"

She fixed a smile on her face, an unconvincing smile if he'd
ever seen one. "Of course I do," she said. "It's an adventure.
I'll see the colonies for myself…well, Virginia…and I'll begin
anew where no one but my aunt knows me." Her cheerful
mien faltered, her smile slipping away. "Even knowing what
trouble I can be, she urged me to come live with her. I hope

I don't make Aunt Rosamond's life harder than it already is."

"I doubt you could." He'd heard what life was like in the colonies, all of the small farms struggling to get by.

Virginia. He couldn't imagine Amelia carrying buckets of water, working the land… Wait, Virginia? "If you were traveling to your aunt in Virginia, why were you on a ship near the West Indies?"

Amelia moved to his other side, the weight of his hair growing lighter with each snip. "Captain Tuttlage and my father are friends. They made the arrangement to have me accompany the captain with the understanding that his shipping route would remain largely the same."

"How far did this route extend?"

"We traveled to Madagascar first before heading this way."

David grimaced. Just the mention of the place put a foul taste in his mouth. All the months he'd spent there as a slave. The humiliation and fury he had tried to forget threatened to rise up like a blister from the raging sun.

"Is something wrong? Oh." She winced and looked down at her hand, a drop of blood forming on the tip of one finger. Irritation marred her features before she raised the offending finger and put it between her lips.

"Let me see." All thoughts of his miserable past faded as he drew the finger from her mouth. A thin cut lined its tip, the blood flow already slowing. The injury would heal quickly without much tending. Still, he wished he could comfort her in some way, not only for the cut, but for the loneliness and despair he'd glimpsed when she spoke of her family, her future. But how? At one time, he'd have easily told a joke or playfully soothed her in some way. Now anything that came to mind seemed awkward and useless.

He contemplated her injury so long, a blush rose to her cheeks, and she pulled her hand away. "I think if a shave is in order, you should do it yourself."

Probably wise advice. While he still didn't accept her theory of bad luck, she certainly suffered more than her share of minor mishaps. He couldn't fathom how someone could be so graceful one moment and maladroit the next. Still, if Amelia could keep him from wallowing in his own miserable past and bring him one whit closer to the man he'd once been, he'd be forever grateful.

· · ·

The next morning, Amelia followed David into the dining area, praying she'd see all the sailors bent to a hearty breakfast. While the room wasn't barren as it had been the prior day, it had plenty of room to spare. The cook slopped rations of oatmeal into bowls and handed one to her and one to David. Taking her bowl, she scanned the room, noting the suspicious looks cast her way and spotted Mr. Rixon along with the rest. She approached one of two long tables and sat across from William, the one soul who greeted her with a smile.

"Good mornin', lovely," he said, as if he hadn't a care that the attention of the room had shifted their way.

David sank onto the bench next to her. "Where are the rest?" he asked William.

William took a bite of his breakfast. "Some are still sick, some asleep. No need for work today."

She'd noticed. Once again not the slightest breeze ruffled

the sails. Although William seemed to think nothing of it, those on the far side of the table near the door eyed her as if she were the very devil himself. No longer hungry, she stirred the watery oats with her spoon.

"A hair trim." William shook his head as he eyed David's newly shorn mane. "You sure like to make trouble for yourself, don't you?"

David cocked his head to the side. "What do you mean?"

"Haven't you heard?" William chuckled. "It's bad luck to trim your hair or nails at sea. It makes Neptune angry, it does."

The look David fixed on William should have set his orange locks to flame. "Hadn't heard that one, and I rightly don't care. Although I do seem to remember one about redheads."

"Do tell me," William begged, a smile playing about his mouth.

David leaned forward and spoke in a hushed voice. "I've heard they should be avoided before boarding a ship, and if that can't be helped, speak to them before they can speak to you."

William laughed. "Ah, now I see why I can never get a word in on dry land."

From the corner of her eye, Amelia watched the men sitting nearest the door while she pretended to sample her breakfast. Rixon nudged the crewman next to him, a man missing one finger on his right hand. He spoke up. "Rixon has the right of it. If something isn't done about the woman, we'll be stranded here until our food and water run out."

"The winds have been calm before for far longer," David argued. "Have some patience."

"It's not just the wind," another chimed in. "What of Frederick's legs, of the sickness we all fell prey to?"

"All?" said still another. "Not *all* of us grew sick."

David hadn't, and neither had she. All eyes shifted to where they sat, and a prickle of unease raced over her skin. She thought to defend herself—she had no control over who was affected by her affliction—but that would only confirm their suspicions that she was the cause.

"Here now." An old fellow rose from the bench toward the middle of the table, the same one who'd requested a kiss for luck. "The lass has done nothing to you. If anything, she's lucky to have avoided the illness herself. Who's to say she's not the reason no one's died from it yet? Leave her be."

If it wasn't untoward, she'd kiss that old fellow now. What a kind soul.

Unfortunately, not all felt as she did.

"Sit down, you old fool," the one missing a finger called out.

"Rufus, don't be talking to Bart that way," the cook demanded, throwing his ladle into the pot of oatmeal. "We've been sailing longer than you've been alive."

"Don't mean nothing," someone yelled.

"Shut your gob," another answered.

Soon the room became divided, each side shouting their views of her, of one another, and God knew what else. The man missing his finger landed the first punch, and in a blink, the room erupted in violence. Fists were thrown and daggers drawn, even bowls of oatmeal were smashed into heads.

David grabbed her by the wrist and hauled her toward the door, but the way was blocked. He dodged a fist and used one of his own. Shoving his opponent back, he opened a narrow path to the door. David made a move to drag her through, but the glint of steel stopped him.

"Get to the cabin and lock the door," he said, drawing his assailant away from her. When the path opened once more, he risked a glance her way. "Go!"

She raced ahead, barely slipping past the skirmish. Once through the door, she grasped her petticoats and ran down the corridor. Footsteps followed at a rapid pace. David? She looked back, and her stomach hit the floor. Despite her best efforts, Rixon caught up to her and seized her arm in a bruising grip.

"This has to end," Rixon growled, dragging her onto the main deck and toward the rail. "You have to go."

"Stop!" She dug her heels in and yanked at his hold, only managing to slow him down. "Captain Swain said—"

He shook her hard. "The captain has no idea what lies ahead if I don't do something. You'll be the death of us all."

They reached the rail and Rixon hoisted her up. She kicked and screamed, sure she would soon feel nothing but air, then water. Even if her dress didn't drag her down to the ocean's depths, she couldn't swim. Her heart pounded so hard, it just might burst from her chest and reach the water first. *Think! Do something.*

"If you kill me, you'll die!" she shrieked. The exact words had come unbidden, but they succeeded where nothing else could. Rixon froze in place, his grip still too strong to escape.

"That's how the curse works," she lied, hoping the quaver in her voice didn't give her away.

He set her on her feet and pushed her toward the rail. A healthy glimmer of fear in his eyes, he pulled a dagger from his belt. "Jump," he ordered.

Was he insane? Her hip against the rail, she stood defiant. "I won't do it."

Rixon muttered an oath. "You don't belong here. You're endangering us all." He thrust the dagger forward, threatening to stab her. "Return to your home, siren."

"Amelia!" David raced toward them, followed by William and several others.

Rixon's eyes rounded, and desperation flared bright. With a bellow, he lunged, his arms outstretched. In the scant seconds that passed, she launched herself to the side, but not far enough. Rixon grabbed her, his momentum propelling them both to the top of the rail. She screamed and twisted, shoving him away with all her strength. His grasp on her slipped, and she scrambled for a hold on the ship as he tumbled over the side and into the water below.

David seized her by the sides and set her back on her feet, then clasped her to him. "My God. Are you hurt?" he asked.

She shook her head, unable to speak. Her legs shook so badly, she would have dropped to the planks if not for David.

The crewman with the missing finger made a move to climb over the rail, but William stopped him with a hard yank.

"Use your noggin, Rufus," he warned. "The fall alone would kill you."

Rufus glanced over the rail, then gave a growl of frustration. "To the boats!"

The men hurried away, leaving her with David and a sick feeling in her middle. She leaned over and peered at the surface of the water below. No sign of Rixon.

Her hair bristled, starting at the nape of her neck and rising to her crown. Tears blurred her vision, and she shook all the more. Rixon was likely dead. A sob tore free at what she'd just witnessed, at what could have happened. Did the crew think as Rixon had? Did they want to kill her? She drew in a sharp breath. Would they blame her for Rixon's death?

David guided her face toward his and looked into her eyes. "Don't cry. You're safe now. I won't let anything happen to you."

She trusted David. She truly did, and still the tears fell. How long could he defend her against a determined crew? And what price would he pay in the process?

"What's the trouble?" Captain Swain called from an upper deck.

David squeezed her tightly before he answered, "Man overboard."

"Who is it?" The captain surveyed the waters where a boat now floated. Rufus dove in.

"Rixon," David called back.

A mixture of suspicion and surprise flickered across the captain's face. "I'll be down," he said, turning away from them to head for the stairs.

David brushed the tears from her cheeks. "The captain will help. He can keep the crew in line."

To protect one woman? She found that hard to believe.

The captain soon approached them. "What happened?"

Despite his words of reassurance, David stepped forward, blocking Amelia from view. "I have witnesses who can attest that Rixon fell overboard as he attacked Miss Archer."

Captain Swain looked over David's shoulder with a

critical stare, and her pulse leaped.

David tensed. "She had nothing to do with—"

The captain raised a hand. "Rixon was a mutinous fop who has done nothing but make trouble since he boarded our ship. Good riddance, I say." He moved to David's side, his gaze returning to her. "Besides, if a mere slip of a girl could kill him, Rixon deserved to die."

A clap of fabric overhead drew their attention toward the sky as a sudden breeze filled the mainsail.

"It appears our luck has changed." Captain Swain raised his hands to cup his mouth and yelled to the men below. "Back to the ship, men. Look lively. We've got work to do."

"Come, Amelia." David guided her from the rail. "I'll take you to your cabin."

She let him escort her away as the captain disappeared through a door that led below decks.

"Maybe with Rixon gone, we'll finally have some peace."

David's words fell flat. They both knew that wouldn't be the case. Rixon had died in his attempt to kill her, and there would be some who would say his death gave testament to the truth of his claims. Now that the seed of superstition had been planted, it was only a matter of time before the crew acted on their fears.

Chapter Five

This time I won't escape. None of us will.

Amelia gasped and held onto the bedpost as the ship rode another ocean swell. The floor slanted at an unwieldy angle and her feet slipped beneath her. She winced from the pain in her ankle. She'd removed her heeled slippers long ago, but not before twisting her ankle as she tried to remain upright.

Nausea gripped her, and she stared out the small window. As if Neptune was releasing his fury, the seas rolled and heaved. She'd never seen such immense waves. They dwarfed the ship, concealed the horizon, and blotted out the sun. The force of the wind clouded the sky with a hazy mist. How quickly the seas had changed from morning to afternoon.

A chill sank deep into her skin as the rush of water grew louder to her ears, drowning out all else. The cabin lurched in the opposite direction, taking her stomach with it. *The ship will not sink. A wave will not flip it onto its side…*

A knock rattled the door.

Her racing heart tripped over itself. They'd come for her. The captain's mercy had come to an end, and to save themselves, they would cast her overboard.

"Amelia?"

David's voice. Thank heavens.

"Amelia, let me in."

A short, hysterical laugh erupted from her throat. He wanted her to cross the room and unlock the door with the ship swaying like a drunken sailor? The instant the ship became somewhat level, she limped to the door, barely making the three steps before the floor leaned again. She clasped the door handle, but still fell to one knee with a whimper.

The sound must have carried. Something heavy banged against the door, or rather someone. "Amelia!"

"Stop. I'm fine. I'm fine." Fumbling with the key in her pocket, she pushed herself to her feet, then unlocked the door.

Before she could open it herself, David pushed the door wide. The ship pitched, and she stumbled, her ankle almost giving out again. David caught her arm and hauled her back, his feet planted wide to keep his balance. His arms encircled her waist.

She latched onto him, clasping him around the middle and pressing her face against his chest. "We're going to sink, aren't we?"

"From a few waves? No. Enough of the crew have recovered from their illness to man the posts. They'll keep this ship afloat, I promise you."

His voice was calm and sure even as another wave rocked them so hard he too staggered across the floor. He seized a bedpost and brought her to the bed to sit down beside him.

"I came to make sure you had no candles lit," he said with a wink.

No candles? She hadn't the breath to laugh at his joke. It seemed all the air in the cabin was gone. "We're going to die, and it's my fault," she murmured, growing lightheaded from the constant motion.

He pulled her closer to his side and gave her a squeeze. "We are not going to die."

"We are." When the ship lurched at a steep angle once more, she had nothing to hold onto but David. She clung to him, an arm around his neck and another at his waist, her head against his shoulder. Rixon had been right. "I should have been left behind. I'm bad luck." *Oh, why did I decide to visit my aunt?*

"I don't believe that, and neither should you."

"But—"

"I never took you for arrogant."

Arrogant? She lifted her head, ready to insist he explain himself, but stopped at his widening grin.

"Do you really think you're so powerful that you can coax an ocean to toss us about?"

"No, I...I've always been told..." She looked into his eyes, his skepticism plain to see. He still didn't understand even after all that had happened. "Bad things happen all the time." She leaned with the ship, her weight pushing into him, and his arm around her tightened.

"So you've said."

She lifted up her bare hand for him to see. "I have the scars to prove it."

"Show me."

Angling her hand to display the back of her thumb, she

ran a finger over a glossy splotch. "This burn is from candle wax."

David chuckled. "Why doesn't that surprise me?"

She ignored his quip. "And this," she pointed out a fingernail with a white mark already beginning to form, "is from dropping the lid of my trunk onto my hand just this morning."

"It proves nothing, except that you may be clumsy." He shook his head. "Next you'll tell me the faint mark on your cheek was caused by a terrible accident while brushing your hair."

She rubbed the spot in question. She remembered it well. Her stepmother had given it to her when she'd lost her temper. She'd slapped Amelia, and her ring had left its mark. Frustration welled up like a bubble about to burst. What was wrong with her? What pitiful examples. She could do better, much better. "My younger sister walks with a cane because of me. She fell down the stairs rushing to greet me when I returned from running away from home after an argument with my stepmother...and," she yanked on the fabric covering her shoulder, but couldn't move it quite far enough, "I was accidentally shot by a musket when I was a child playing in the—"

When a cavernous groan rose up from the bowels of the ship, all further examples fled her mind. Fear lanced through her, and every muscle tensed until she shook.

"Pay no attention to that sound," David told her. "*The Wanderer* is solidly built. It will survive these waves."

Amelia heard him as if at a distance. Lies meant to keep her calm. They were sure to die. She could feel it deep in her bones.

He bowed his head to capture her attention. "Amelia. Look at me."

She couldn't. The vessel bellowed its misery again, and her heart nearly stopped beating. How long did they have left before the ship broke apar—

His mouth, firm and warm, pressed against hers, silencing her fears. No peck on the lips, his kiss penetrated her senses, bringing her back to the here and now. In this moment, she was safe in his arms and there was nowhere else she wanted to be. She sank into him, surrendering herself to his command, and luxuriating in the—

He pulled away all too soon.

His soft brown eyes studied her face, his gaze trailing over her lips for the longest minute. "Nothing is going to happen to you. These rough seas will pass."

Although a thread of fear remained, a more pleasant sensation surpassed it. A giddy rush of excitement danced in her belly unlike anything she'd ever experienced. David stirred some sweet emotion within her she couldn't define, but she longed to feel it again. She leaned forward and settled her mouth on his. He froze as if unsure what to do.

Fire leaped to her middle when his lips finally moved. With a moan, he deepened the kiss, his mouth exploring and savoring, and that feeling of exhilaration returned. She placed her hand on his chest and marveled at the smooth skin so hot to her touch, then brushed higher along his neck, past the stubble on his jaw, and on to feather-soft hair that teased her fingers.

His tongue swept across her lips in a sensual glide that made her shiver, and she opened her mouth to do the same. The brush of tongue on tongue awakened a need within her she didn't understand. Her muscles softened and melted, molding her more intimately against him, her breasts pressed to his side.

David tensed and drew back, his breathing heavy. "We should stop."

The rise and fall of the ship became noticeable again, but it didn't frighten her as much as before. "You kissed me first," she said, her mind in a pleasure-filled daze.

His strong arms still supported her against the swells, but he'd put more space between them. "Yes. To keep your mind from your fears."

She tensed, and her cheeks grew uncomfortably warm. Was that all the kiss had been? A tactic to keep her from panic? With a heartfelt glare, she pushed his arm from her and rose to her feet, grasping the bedpost to steady herself. "Next time leave me be. I'd rather be frightened." Now who was fibbing?

Oh, what was she thinking? She should be happy he had no interest in her. He was wrong about her. She was bad luck, and those who stayed too close suffered. David was a kind soul who'd come to her aid when no one else would. He would be far better off if she kept him at a distance. Yes. She should be happy. Instead, she yearned for what she could never have.

• • •

His back against the cabin door and his rear firmly planted on the floor planks, David stared at Amelia asleep in the bed. The waves had subsided hours ago. Now the sun barely lit the gloomy morning sky. A restless sleeper, Amelia had lost her cap and her hair had come unpinned. The long blond waves half obscured her face. How he longed to brush them aside to reveal her expressive features and to kiss those luscious lips again.

Something about her drew him in like a siren's song. She was beautiful in the extreme, and graceful, when she wasn't poking slivers in her skin or burning herself alive. Perhaps her slight frame and her penchant for trouble were what appealed so strongly to his protective instincts. Possibly, although deep down he sensed something more. Amelia was a gentle soul who tried to see the good in people no matter their actions. Just as he used to.

If only he could return to those days of naiveté. Life had been enjoyable then. Now everything tasted of bitterness. His innocence and compassion were long gone. All that he'd lived through this past year had jaded him to the point he barely recognized the man he'd become. A sweet girl like Amelia deserved more than he could offer.

Someone banged on the door so hard, his back bounced from the force. Amelia's eyes sprang open, and she pushed herself upright, her hair tumbling past her shoulders.

"Who goes?" David asked as he sprang to his feet.

"Rufus, amongst others."

Rufus. His presence didn't bode well. David pulled his dagger from its sheath, dread tightening his grip. "What's your business?"

"Open the door, or we'll break it down," Rufus warned.

If that swine thought he could give orders here…

"Cap'n Swain wants to see you and the lass," another voice chimed in. William?

He turned toward the bed. As quick and efficient as only a woman could, Amelia secured her hair in a knot at the back of her head. Despite the fear in her eyes, she issued a nod as if she'd expected this outcome. Honestly, he had as well. After the men had returned to the ship and a short prayer had been said for Rixon, the swells had come on so suddenly, there had been no time for accusations. Even with the captain's acceptance of Rixon's death, the crew would demand, at the very least, an explanation. A sense of foreboding clawed its way up his spine.

When Amelia pinned her lace cap in place and stepped forward, he had the urge to tell the men outside to hie off, but he couldn't defend this small cabin from a whole ship of pirates with one sword and a dagger, especially if Captain Swain played a part. Instead, he unlocked the door and swung it open, his blade raised.

Rufus stood in the fore with a belligerent mien and stance. Behind him, William gave a sheepish look.

Three had come to the door. David ignored all save Rufus. "Back away."

Rufus's eyes narrowed, but he complied, retreating a few paces.

David held out a hand to Amelia. "Come with me."

She didn't hesitate. She stepped forward and stayed close to his side as he ventured into the hall, careful to keep Rufus in his sight.

The three men led the way to the deck where Captain Swain and the rest of the crew awaited them. Once more the air was motionless. The sails hung as slack as they had the days prior to the swells. Damnation. How could that possibly be?

"Now that David and Miss Archer are present, let the trial begin," the captain called out with the agreeable expression of a man eager to be entertained.

"Trial?" David asked as they came to stand before the captain. "What's this?"

"She has to go," someone shouted.

"She's going to kill us all," another joined in.

The crew gathered in a loose circle around them, and David looked from one man to the next. Although their agitation was apparent, he detected no immediate threat. "I fought Rixon so she could stay," David announced. "Captain's orders."

"Sorry, lad." Captain Swain said. "She has the crew at odds, and I'll not have mutiny on this ship. Now put away your blade. This will be decided without blood."

David resheathed his dagger, for now, although the unease that had clawed up his spine now weighed on his chest like a two ton anchor. "What then? You'll throw her overboard to appease a horde of superstitious fools?"

Amelia sidled closer, her face pinched by fear.

Captain Swain smiled. "I'm not so coldhearted as that. We'll have a trial, then the crew will vote to decide her fate." He gestured toward David. "Never fear. You may speak on her behalf, and those who choose to take part can have their say either for or against."

A trial? This was nothing but a sham. Before David could voice an objection, Rufus stepped forward. "Rixon is dead because of this woman."

"She didn't kill him," David argued. "He fell overboard while attempting murder."

A few nods from witnesses attested to the truth. He wasn't alone in this.

Rufus held his arms wide and appealed to his brethren. "Nay, Rixon sacrificed himself to save us. He gave up his life trying to rid us of the witch who stands before us now."

Such tripe. Rufus spewed as much nonsense as Rixon had. "Stow your drivel. She's no more a witch than you are."

"Rixon told us all that had happened on *Fortune's Song* because of her, and you've seen for yourself the effects here. No wind to buffet our sails and illness throughout our ranks."

"Both of which we've experienced before without Amelia on board," David reminded him. "Neither were her doing. No one can control nature or what you fools eat and drink."

"Waves nearly as high as the ship's tallest sail, and wind so strong, rigging snapped like thread," Rufus declared, undaunted.

"Aye. You have the right of it," someone yelled as others muttered in agreement.

"How could she have possibly caused the ocean to heave?" David called back. "If anything, I say she's brought us good luck. No one died due to illness, and we survived the swells with the ship intact."

"Not all of us survived the swells. Several of the crew were injured and two washed overboard," Rufus countered.

The majority of the crew spoke up in kind, and their murmurs rose in volume, drowning out those who might disagree.

David turned to William, the one friend he'd made amongst the crew, the one who might help the others listen to reason. William winced and looked away. He wouldn't cross his brethren. This ship and crew meant everything to him.

"During the squall, rum barrels in the hold broke loose and were smashed against the hull," Rufus bellowed. "Most of our water, too."

Amelia's gloved hand snatched hold of David's arm, her breaths quick and shallow.

"We'll die of thirst," a crewman shouted to be heard

above the din.

David palmed the hilt of his sword, the faces around him too eager. "She had nothing—"

"And look you now, not a wisp of breeze again," Rufus added. "If she stays, we could languish here for weeks."

A clamor of assent rose up, with a few voices louder than the rest. "She's bad luck. Best be rid of her." Rufus's supporters crowded in. They needed no official verdict to know they'd won.

David began to draw his sword. He'd vowed to protect her, and he'd defend her as long as he could.

"No." With a hand on his, Amelia stopped him from pulling the weapon from its sheath. "It's no use. You can't fight them all."

She trembled and sweat beaded on her brow, yet the conviction in her voice and bearing attested to an inner strength.

"I'll leave," she said to the captain. "All I ask is that you allow me the use of your rowboat, and give me a few provisions."

Amelia held her chin high, facing the captain with courage and an outward calm despite the circumstances. She must know, with or without a boat, the crew had sentenced her to death. All that remained to be decided was whether it would be quick or slow.

A note of admiration flickered over Captain Swain's features as if he, too, couldn't help but respect her bravery. "You may take the small wherry we salvaged from *Fortune's Song*. As for provisions though, we have none to share."

The crew didn't object. Pirates they may be, but cutthroats who would murder a defenseless woman? None of them could do it outright. No, they would send her off in a rowboat in the middle of an ocean to die of thirst and starvation. The thought churned his stomach. "I'll go with her." The words spilled from his mouth unbidden, but once out, he knew he'd stand by them. Nothing else would do.

Amelia blanched. "No, you won't."

He gazed into her eyes. The fear in their depths was too bright to ignore. "I'll go with you."

She shook her head. "You don't know what you're saying."

"You'd have us lose our musician?" the captain asked, his question sharp.

David drilled the man with a glare. "I'll never play for you again, either way." While they could physically force him to stay, he'd rather break his violin to pieces than entertain this lot again.

Captain Swain's mouth twitched as he scanned the crew before him. Musicians were hard to come by. Still, what good was one who refused to play? "So be it," he finally said.

"Don't do this, David," William warned in a harsh whisper.

William had been a friend from the first, until today. His actions, or lack thereof, proved how shallow his friendship ran.

David grasped Amelia's hand. His decision was final. "We go together."

"No." She pulled her hand away. "I won't let you."

Her show of spunk only strengthened his will. She was worth defending, worth saving, or sacrificing himself in the attempt. He faced her, towering over her by several inches. "How will you stop me?"

She let out an outraged huff. "By tying you down if I have to." With that, she strode from him. To where, he had no idea. To find rope? Despite everything, he smiled. Would she really attempt to tie him up? A small gleeful part of him rather hoped she would.

Chapter Six

With David's assistance, Amelia stepped inside the rowboat and quickly sat before she tipped it over, fell, or in some other way managed to drown herself. "Don't come with me," she pleaded once more. She'd appealed to the captain, to William, to anyone who'd listen, asking them to help her keep David aboard. All to no success. While *she* couldn't physically restrain him, *they* could have if they'd tried. None were willing. Blast them all.

David deftly climbed in and sat facing her, an amused smile on his lips. "If you keep saying that, you'll hurt my feelings."

She released a long breath, the tickling of relief making her guilt that much worse. They'd been given no drink, the crew declaring that what they had left couldn't be spared, and no food—why share food when she and David would likely die of thirst far quicker than hunger? Even her things had been left behind. The captain had told her she wouldn't need them for long.

All they had was David's violin, which no one else could play, a pistol, a flask of gunpowder, and two shot.

David untied the boat and took up the oars, following the captain's instructions to row from the ship in short order.

"Do you still want to defend the crew?" he asked as if he sensed where her thoughts had turned.

She glanced up at the rail where several men watched them row away. "I'd rather not be banished from their ship, but I don't blame them for what they've done."

David huffed out a sound of disgust. "How can you forgive them so readily? They blamed you for things out of your control."

"I've grown used to being blamed." She'd come to expect it, and nothing could compare to the sorrow of leaving her family in order to keep them safe. Even after six months of travel, the ache wouldn't abate. Maybe it never would.

"Yes. Your stepmother." David rowed with long, swift strokes, quickly widening the distance between them and the pirate ship. "Did your father not defend you, tell your stepmother to hold her tongue?"

"He did." She remembered the arguments. "My stepmother insisted she simply spoke the truth and that his love for me blinded him to what was really happening." Despite it all, he had loved her dearly, he and her stepsister both had.

"She sounds like a shrew. How can you believe her over your father?"

A pitiful laugh rose up. "I've been in six carriage accidents over the course of my life; my family is prone to choking on food or even their own saliva; my father fell from his horse shortly after seeing me in the wood, injuring his back; my family became sick with the measles—the only house in town to have such issue; my governess was stung—"

"Stop." David shook his head. "You didn't cause any of those things. They could have happened in anyone's household. It's simply…" His brows drew low.

"Bad luck," she finished for him. "Exactly. That's why I left." Everyone she came in contact with was at risk, including David. After all, her own mother had died giving birth to her. "Why did you come with me?" she asked, more determined than ever. "There was no need. You can't save me, but you could have saved yourself… You still can." If they returned to the ship, the crew might welcome him back.

David stopped rowing and her heart gave a lurch. Maybe he'd finally listen. Maybe he would leave her.

He grinned and reached behind for something tucked inside his shirt. When his hand reappeared, he held a modest-sized bowl. He set it on the floor of the boat and looked to the murky sky. "If we're lucky, we'll have rainwater to drink soon enough."

Lucky? Was he daft? "David, you should go back."

He peered at the pirate ship in the distance. "Few will miss me." He picked up the oars again. "Possibly none."

Her frustration mounted. Why wouldn't he listen? She wanted to gnash her teeth and shout at him until he understood the predicament he'd put himself in, but she battled to curb her temper, a side of herself she showed no one, not anymore.

Putting up a fuss would do no good anyway. Clearly, David had made up his mind and wouldn't be swayed. Instead, she focused on what he'd said last. *Few will miss me.* How was that possible? Then again, he had opposed them at every turn, for her sake. "How long did you sail with them?"

"Just shy of eight months."

"That long, and you've made no friends?" Perhaps that was the way with pirates.

"I never truly got on with that lot," he explained.

"Then why did you become one of them?"

His expression turned somber, and he said no more.

A splotch of rain landed on her nose, then on her cheek. She looked to the dark skies, the cool touch of the droplets refreshing.

David adjusted the bowl to lay level. "See now, you are good luck." He tucked his violin beneath his seat, but as the drizzle turned into a shower, she held out her hand.

"Give it to me."

He passed to her the worn instrument, and she tucked it beneath her petticoats to keep it dry. Interesting that he would protect the violin when he claimed he no longer loved to play. Indeed, why had he brought it along at all? David hid his emotions well, although obviously something troubled him deeply. Whether he would ever divulge his secrets, she couldn't say, but they'd have a few days left if he chose to share his thoughts.

His dark hair already clinging to his forehead, David rowed, but to where? The wind and waves had thrown *The Wanderer* off course. Even the pirates had yet to determine where they were. Shielding her eyes from the rain, Amelia stared out at the endless blue water that surrounded them. The rain soaked her dress, adding to its weight, a weight that grew more oppressive the longer she contemplated their fate.

The breeze picked up, and she looked back to watch the ship's sails billow, further proving to all aboard that they'd made the right decision to cast her away. No doubt David couldn't return even if he wanted to, now that his crewmates' luck had improved. The pirates would likely fire on them if they dared to come close.

She should be saddened by that fact. And in some ways she was. In other, selfish ways, she was glad to have David here. "Thank you for coming with me."

His eyes warmed and his countenance softened. "My pleasure."

The words of a gentleman. The ache in her chest grew stronger, and deep in her heart, she wept for David's sacrifice. Even with the rain filling the bowl, how long would they last without water? Without food. He would be punished because of her sins.

Uncomfortably warm, Amelia's skin prickled. She groaned and nestled into the comforting cushion beneath her cheek, a steady heartbeat and the splash of waves lulling her back to sleep. Heartbeat? She opened her eyes to the bright light of midday. Her head rested on David's bare chest and her body was half sprawled on top of his. Her face flamed. She pushed herself up and winced. Her back ached from sleeping in the cramped boat.

"She awakes." David squinted at her, holding his shirt above to shield them from the sun.

Her gaze shifted to his lips, lips she'd kissed with such delight in the cabin…until he'd pulled away.

"Is something amiss?" he asked. A fine breeze ruffled his hair, and she fought the urge to feel its softness again.

"No. I'm fine." The sun beat down on them from high in the heavens. Her throat dry and the water they'd collected in the bowl long gone, she crawled to the side of the boat to dip her fingers into the sea. Cupping her hands, she lifted the water to her mouth. At least she could find some relief here.

In a flash of bronze skin, David grasped her hands and pushed them from her mouth. "Don't drink that. It will increase your thirst."

"I only wanted a small taste to wet my throat."

He pointed toward the floor. "There's still rainwater."

She peered down at the shallow channel of water trapped along the center seam of the hull. She'd cringe at the narrow puddle of murky liquid if her throat didn't already burn from thirst. Bending closer, she tried to scoop some into her hands. Too shallow. Blast it. She lifted her hands and licked the moisture from her salty skin. More. She'd use a piece of clothing to sop up the water and wring out into her mouth, but it would absorb far more than it would provide. Enough. Grasping a seat for support, she gave up the ladylike approach and leaned forward. She groaned when her sore muscles protested the movement.

"Do you need help?" David placed an arm around her middle, and a desire to lean into him swamped her.

Where were these unbidden impulses coming from? "No. I—"

Too late. He eased her forward, that arm hugging her close. Her mouth reached the water, and with a sweep of his hand, he brushed back the locks of hair that had escaped her pins. His fingers lightly stroked her scalp as he held her tresses in place, and she momentarily forgot what she was supposed to do.

"Go ahead. Take a drink," he prompted.

She slurped a taste and more. The gritty liquid coated her tongue, but she drank down her share, ignoring the musty flavor, the entire time her senses focused solely on the man holding her in place.

"Had enough?"

"Yes, thank you." She wiped her mouth. The scant moisture didn't slake her thirst, yet it would have to do. "Your turn."

With a nod, David bent low, but stopped short when she gasped.

On his lower back, a scar in the shape of a groove marred his skin. She couldn't help herself. She reached out. When her fingers came into contact with the old wound, he flinched.

"What is this scar from?"

He peered at her over his shoulder. "It's nothing."

"How can you say that? It looks like the wound was grave." A thought dawned. "Did the pirates do this to you?" Was that why he had no great affinity toward them?

His attention returned to the bottom of the boat with a soft curse. "No. It happened before I joined up."

"Then who?"

He held his silence.

She withdrew her hand and curbed her tongue. Who was she to pry? If he didn't want to tell her, she had no right to ask.

David bent forward. His mouth on the water's surface, he sipped from the pool as if savoring a lover's kiss. The memory of his warm mouth on hers flooded her mind, and excitement leaped inside her, the sensation not unwelcome, if inappropriate. She tore her gaze away from his lips. Avoiding his back and its scar, she looked lower where his breeches tightened over his bent legs and well-formed backside.

Oh, my. Her stomach fluttered like ripples on the ocean's surface. Amelia swallowed and nearly choked on her own wayward thoughts.

David settled onto his side and held up his shirt for shade, motioning for her to join him. Calming her racing heart, she lay down next to him, the feel of his arm around her still vivid in her mind. *Stop. No more lascivious thoughts.*

Then again, why not? She always worried about what her affliction would do to those who got too close, but what more could she do to David? They'd likely die within the week, possibly sooner. Why not enjoy what little time they had left?

Her nerves quaked with the possibility, even as she inwardly grimaced. She had no experience in the matter of men. She heaved a sigh of frustration and leaned back. Lustful thoughts were all fine and good, but to act on them… She had no idea how.

David's meager shelter shadowed their faces, but her body burned as if she were on fire. She fanned her bodice where too much skin lay exposed to the sun. Hot to the touch, her chest had already turned pink. His eyes followed her movements. "You'll need to shield yourself from the sun, or you'll burn further."

A fine idea, if they had more shade available. "How would I do that?"

He glanced up toward his shirt and cocked one brow.

Despite herself, a wicked thrill lanced through her. "You…you'd have me strip down?"

"I'll be a perfect gentleman." His expression of innocence didn't deceive her. Not when his barely suppressed smile alluded to more.

Sweat trickled down her neck and between her breasts. Did she dare? She sweltered in her heavy blue gown.

"Would you rather blister?" he asked, his tone suggesting this whole discussion was a silly one.

She glanced down at her pinkened skin. She *was* being silly. What good was propriety when it meant burning up? After all, they were far beyond society's scorn now. Even the pirate ship had disappeared. *Why not be comfortable and free? Why not be bold and adventurous?*

"You're right." Allowing her skin to blister would do her no good. Clearing her throat, she rose to her knees, unpinned her stomacher, and stopped.

David watched the progress of her fingers intently, his eyes giving off more heat than the sun.

With a twinge of self-consciousness, she clasped the loose fabric to her chest, her heart beating against her fingertips. Perhaps this was a bad idea.

"My apologies." A smile tugged at his mouth, and he turned to look out at the horizon stretching as far as the eye could see.

Better, but better still, she moved to face away from him, careful not to rock the boat. She fumbled with the fastenings and removed the yards of fabric. Her skin instantly cooled without the added bulk, and her spirits rose. The impulsive, scandalous act of undressing awakened all her senses, and with satisfaction, she sank down on the other side of the tiny boat. In only her stays, shift, petticoats, hose, and shoes, she raised her gown above her head to shade her exposed skin, resting her elbows on the sides of the boat, then basked in the slight breeze that touched her.

"Cooler?" he asked.

Adjusting her position on the hard planks, she nodded. "Yes. Much." She shifted her grip on the gown in her hands, casting a longer shadow over herself. Across from her, David baked in the sun. His shirt did little to shade more than his face and neck. She worried her lip as guilt gnawed its way through what was left of her scruples. She was half naked, after all.

"What about you?" she finally asked. "Your chest will burn."

His eyes brightened. "What are you proposing?"

"I can share the shelter of my gown if you'd like."

With a grin that melted her insides like warm honey, he moved toward her end of the small boat. "How can I refuse such a generous offer?" Settling down beside her, he took up one end of the gown.

She peered out at the sparkling waves, the sun gleaming down from the heavens above, and felt David's regard as plainly as if he slid his hand along the side of her body.

Amelia couldn't resist. She peeked over at him.

"You appear to be enjoying yourself," he said, the expression on his face one of curiosity.

"Why shouldn't I?" She'd never asked for this affliction. And while she pitied every poor soul affected, she certainly didn't wish to die. In fact, her predicament had taught her the value of the present. "Every moment is precious because you never know what could happen in the next." Even now, she couldn't help but appreciate the blue of the ocean and the welcome company of the man beside her.

David's eyes softened, and a look of introspection drained away the last of his youthful spirit. "I used to believe that, too."

"Used to?"

He studied the water around them, and a trace of sadness permeated the air. "At one time, all I cared about was playing my violin." His lips twitched in a fleeting smile. "I'd travel around town, meet new people, and play my music."

The reverence in his voice… He must have cherished those times. "What made you stop?"

"My father." His attention came back to her, his stare so earnest, as if he had to make her understand. "He hated my playing, or rather what he thought it was doing to me."

"What was it doing?"

"Turning me into a weak man with no concern for the future." David shook his head. "He wanted me to work for the family business."

"And what business would that be?"

"Shipping. My grandfather started the company, one of the largest in all of London, and after he passed on, my father took over. Through his leadership, Lamont Shipping thrived, and now he's looking to his sons to take up the reins."

"What of your brothers?" Her arm growing tired, she shifted to rest it on the edge of the boat.

"I have only one. James has sailed for as long as I can remember. He'd rather be at sea than running the company at home."

"Your father has no issue with that?"

"He does. They've fought about it for years, but James has done his part to expand the business, establishing more port contacts and recommending better sailing routes. Which leaves me, the family disappointment, for my father to mold into his image."

She still didn't understand. "You became a pirate to rebel?"

"Hardly." Taking her lead, he set his elbow on the rim of the boat, making their shelter smaller, more intimate. "I resisted for years, and I thought my father might finally relent… He didn't. Especially after I left home for a fortnight to wander the countryside and play my music." He glanced at her bodice, his gaze remaining for a few long breaths before he adjusted his hold to better shade her skin. "When I returned, my father was livid. To him, my adventure had proven once and for all that something had to be done. We fought with more venom than we ever had, until I grew weary of it. James convinced me to try sailing. He hoped I might enjoy the travel and playing my violin. And for a time, it would appease my father. Perhaps he would see I wasn't a complete sluggard."

"Do you enjoy life at sea?"

"In some ways. Going wherever the wind takes me is a kind of freedom, I suppose."

"But *The Wanderer* is a pirate ship. I doubt that's what he had in mind."

He laughed, soft and low. "You would be right on that count." David sat back and stared straight ahead. "I sailed on one of my father's ships, the next one out, in fact, eager to finally be free of his scorn." A slight scowl dragged his mouth into a frown. "A month into the journey, the ship was captured by pirates. They took all our cargo…and me, a musician, to entertain them."

Oh. She'd had no idea that the men they'd just left… He must have read her thoughts, for he clarified, "It wasn't *The Wanderer's* crew who captured me."

Then who? The question was foremost in her mind, but she held her silence. The anguish on David's face stopped her from saying more.

"Given all that's happened since then, I've begun to wonder if my father is right about me. I don't deserve his respect."

The torment evident in his words cut deep. She lifted her free hand to cradle his cheek and urged him to meet her eyes. "Since I've met you, you've been nothing but kind. You've defended me, comforted me, and stood by my side against a whole ship of pirates. They might have pushed me overboard if it hadn't been for you. You have my undying respect and always will."

David opened his mouth, likely to argue. She silenced him with a finger on his lips. "Your actions are that of an honorable man, one who deserves the utmost respect from all."

He drew her hand away. "Amelia—"

"No. No more." Pressing her mouth to his, she silenced him. His lips were soft, and they moved over hers with hunger and a desperation she wasn't prepared for. Frightening and exhilarating, his kisses captivated. Her temperature rose to match the heat of the day, and her insides liquefied into a puddle. What had started as an impetuous act quickly turned into a frenzy of tongues and mouths.

Her fingers slipped into his hair and she leaned closer, her head pleasantly dizzy and her breath escaping with a groan.

David's lips stilled, and he made a sound halfway between a moan and a curse. He pulled back, and his soulful eyes searched her face, his features drawn in a mask of regret. He still believed himself unworthy. That much was clear. *Oh, David.* When would he stop seeing himself through his father's eyes?

Amelia grasped his free hand in hers and intertwined their fingers.

"I will eventually convince you of your integrity and virtue," she vowed, squeezing his hand for good measure. She only prayed they survived long enough to see the deed done.

Chapter Seven

David drew his violin bow across the strings in soothing strokes. The music, slow and mournful, matched the pensive mood of the boat. The starry sky reminded him of his nights in Madagascar, sleeping in the open. It was a wonder he'd managed to hold onto the scuffed instrument during his days of slavery. Then again, none of the natives had known how to play. His violin would have been of no use to them. Better to threaten to take it from him if he didn't do as they bid...and force him to be their entertainment. Interesting how an act that had once brought such joy had turned into something so loathsome.

And yet, although he didn't have the love for music he once had, playing for Amelia was more satisfying than he'd expected. She lay on the other side of the boat, disheveled but beautiful. Wisps of her straight, blond hair had escaped her pins to frame her face, and her clothes were wrinkled. Still, she had never looked so lovely.

Despite the reduced heat of night, her gown remained on the bottom of the boat, the pace of the day eroding her modesty. Amelia closed her eyes with a peaceful look on her face. She stayed that way for the longest time, until he wondered if she'd fallen asleep, but when she opened her eyes, she stared at him in curiosity. "What were you like, before you set sail…when you roamed about, playing your violin?"

Those days seemed like such a long time ago. His chin on the smooth wood, he continued to draw his bow over the strings, the instrument an extension of himself. "Like you, I appreciated the small things in life. The sun, the rain, the sound of my music." His hand stilled, and he studied the scratches marring the polished wood as his thoughts returned to the many arguments he'd had with his father. "I didn't worry about the future, how I would make enough money for my old age. I lived minute to minute, traveling all over London, and trusted that I'd find some way to keep from going hungry and a place to rest my head." He looked at Amelia as she listened intently. "I trusted people. I laughed more."

She smiled. "I thought trusting people was foolish."

David smiled back, his mood lifting. "It can be." He lowered the violin to his lap. "The truth is that I see glimpses of my old self in you, and a part of me wanted to protect you because I couldn't bear to see someone else lose their love of life."

Amelia sat up, her head tilted to the side. "And the other part?"

"Other part?"

She flung her hands in the air as if frustrated by the

question, but humor glinted in her eyes. "You said that a part of you wanted to protect me because you saw glimpses of yourself in me. What about the other part? I assume it wanted to protect me, too."

Her cheerful disposition, despite their predicament, was amazing. After two days without food and a day without water, she must be suffering just as he was, and still she teased. A slow smile crossed his lips. "The other part of me was mesmerized by your beauty."

In the pale moonlight her cheeks pinkened, and her eyes gleamed playfully. "You jest at my expense."

"Not at all." He set down the violin and shifted closer. "You're as lovely as a flower in the stark of winter... Your hair is the color of wheat under the midday sun, and your eyes—"

"Yes, yes. My eyes are like the sea or the sky or some such nonsense," she quipped with a laugh, the lilting sound like the finest music, better than anything he could ever play.

He sat next to her and stared into those blue-green eyes she made light of. "Very well. You are also extraordinary, forgiving and caring..."

She tilted her head up, and leaned in. "If I'm so very impressive, then kiss me."

He reared away, damning himself for wanting to give in to her request. "I shouldn't."

Amelia moved closer, her hand settling on the side of his face. "Why not? I'm asking you to."

"You deserve a better man than me."

"You *are* a good man, David. Besides," she scanned the opposite side of the boat and back, "I think it's safe to say that you are the best man here."

A chuckle squelched his next breath. "How endearing, and entirely irrelevant."

Her lips pursed and her shoulders dropped. "We're likely to die out here, just the two of us." She lowered her gaze to her knotted fingers. "Before I do, I want to experience as much as I can."

Sadness and understanding tugged at his heart. "We are not going to die." At the incredulous look that creased her brow, he shrugged. "Our situation may seem dire, but I'm not ready to give up all hope." Life held surprises, at least it had for him. Who was to say a ship wouldn't find them? Merchantmen and pirate alike sailed this route to the West Indies all the time.

She shook her head. "Even if we are saved, what man would dare get close to me once he knew the danger?"

"There will be a man for you someday—"

"You don't know that," she insisted, the pain in her voice heartbreaking. "If it were me, I'd stand clear."

Had her thirst and hunger gone to her head? Any man would be fortunate to have her. "Amelia…" He stopped short at the misery that blanketed her features. No matter what he said, she truly thought no man would ever want her. His gut clenched at the thought. He had to make her understand how special she was. She had to know… He brought his hand to the back of her neck and drew her close, his mouth capturing hers in an emphatic kiss, one he hoped would get through to her where no words could.

They'd shared kisses before, but this time he surrendered. No more thoughts of the bitter man he'd become, of how Amelia deserved better than him. Instead, he immersed himself in the feel of her soft lips, her wet tongue, her sweet flavor.

Her arms circled his neck, and she pressed her chest to his, inflaming his senses even more. He grazed his mouth across her cheek and savored the spot just below her ear. "How can you believe that any man could resist you?" he groaned, his hands aching to explore her curves. He wished nothing more than to taste every succulent inch of her skin.

She shivered, her hands delving into his hair. He grasped one of her wrists and nipped a path along the inside of her arm, holding her still as she squirmed from the sensation.

Her breath quickened as he nibbled her wrist, then each of her fingers in turn. When he bent to her palm, he hesitated. He'd given her the kiss she'd sought. He should stop.

"David?" Amelia searched his face. "Please." Her hands skimmed over his bare chest in an invitation he should ignore.

"You wanted a kiss."

"At first," she agreed. "Now I want…" She drew her plump lower lip between her teeth. "I want more."

He stifled a moan as his body tightened in response. "You can't make a request like that without…" He couldn't finish that thought. No man had that kind of restraint. "How much more?"

"Everything," she said, her whisper riding the length of his back and settling in his groin.

Dear God.

Her hands slid over his hips, and a blush rose to her cheeks as they came to rest on his bottom. "I may never get another chance."

Never…another…chance. His mind couldn't comprehend as his body demanded he take action. He crushed her to him and took possession of her mouth with the raw need to pleasure her, to pleasure himself, to finally be free of his own discontent. Perhaps, most of all, to live moment to moment as he'd once done.

Blindly, he pulled out the pins securing her hair. The silken strands washed over his fingertips like a spring rainfall. Her slender body so close to his drove every thought from his head. Gentle hands stroked his back, gliding over that portion of skin that had grown thick and lost nearly all sensation. Numb to the world around him. A bit like him.

In comparison, Amelia was light to his darkness. Sweet and innocent to his bitterness. She wanted to experience the intimacy between a man and a woman, and he would oblige, but he'd best be tender. He'd best slow down.

He rested his forehead against hers to catch his breath and attempt to cool his raging blood.

"Is something the matter?" she asked. "Have I done something wrong?"

He choked on a laugh. "No, love. It's me." Lifting his head, he stared into her beautiful eyes. "You have me burning up from the inside out."

"That's good, isn't it?"

"Aye, but I want to make this as enjoyable for you as possible." He nuzzled her cheek and throat, and felt a tremor run through her. "I want us to savor every minute."

She made a noise halfway between a gasp and a moan. "Just don't savor too long."

"Impossible." He kissed a path lower to the rise of her breasts plumped by her stays. The bounty was too luscious to resist.

Her breath hitched. "If we wait too long, we may be

interrupted."

As he lavished attention on her delectable bosom, he plucked at the laces on her stays, eliciting a short pant with each one. "I'm not the least bit concerned."

"You should be," she stammered. "It could... It could rain."

"We can hope. Rain would be welcome." He rose up to meet her eyes with a quizzical look. "Are you sure you're urging me to go on? Would you rather I stop?"

Her lips curved into a tantalizing smile, all uncertainty dissipating. "I don't want you to stop." She unfastened the ties of her outer petticoat with sure yanks. "I've simply found that my most pleasurable moments are fleeting, at best."

His eyebrows rose. He'd never been accused of being too fleeting when giving pleasure. Not yet. But the way Amelia made him feel...

She released the ties of her under-petticoats next. "Bad circumstances befall me too often to allow for much in the way of happiness." With his help, she wiggled her slender hips out of the voluminous fabric, uncovering the lower half of her shift and a fine pair of stocking-clad legs. "With the exception of today... If one discounts the unbearable heat and the lack of food and water—"

He slid a hand down her leg, effectively silencing her nervous chatter. Beneath her hose, her limb was strong and lissome, almost too thin. How long would she last without food or water? He shoved the thought away. No need to worry about what he couldn't change. Instead, he moved his hand higher, slipping beneath the hem of her shift. She startled when he reached the bare skin of her thigh, then her hip. Soft as the petals of a flower, her skin teased his fingertips as he explored her narrow waist and smooth belly.

She clung to his shoulders as he lowered his mouth to her breasts again, sampling each one. Eager for more, he grasped the strings of her stays with his free hand and pulled to no effect. He made a move to sit, and she strengthened her hold about his shoulders. "Don't stop," she moaned, her hands dropping to free the ties herself. The stiff material soon fell away, and he nipped at a peak through the soft linen of her shift.

Amelia cried out and arched her back. Good God, what an entrancing sight. His groin ached with a need so strong his hands shook. Holding on to what was left of his control, he grazed his fingers over the flesh between her legs, and she whimpered, her hips rising and her thighs opening.

He growled in satisfaction at his first intimate touch. Wet and ready. He caressed and stroked while she writhed beneath him, her chest thrust out in a most enticing way. Gliding his finger into her opening, he captured her cries with his mouth, the heel of his hand applying pressure where she would enjoy it most.

Her hips rocked with his movements, and she reached for his breeches. She attempted to push them down, but he stopped her. "Once these come off, I won't be able to hold back."

"Then don't," she pleaded, her eyes glazed with passion.

"Are you sure?"

That smile returned. "Aye. I'm sure."

Blood surged through his veins as he removed his breeches. The heat of her stare made him harden all the more. When he looked up, she lay before him naked, her pale skin glowing in the moonlight. Her body was perfection, just like the woman within.

A round scar on her shoulder caught his eye, from a gunshot wound, she'd said. He bent over her and kissed the spot. If he had his way, she'd never experience pain again. That thought brought him up short. "There will be some discomfort."

She brought her hand to the side of his face and brushed her lips over his. "I know, and I don't care." She wriggled beneath him, spreading her thighs on either side of his hips, then urged him lower.

The moment he came into contact with her opening, a shudder ran through him. Looking into eyes that showed no fear, he positioned himself and eased inside. Her slick, tight heat almost drove him mad. He resisted the overwhelming desire to thrust deep. *Slow and gentle.* His muscles tensed with need as he pressed himself farther in. Amelia winced when he'd gone halfway, and he paused. "Would you like me to stop?"

She shook her head. "No, go quick. I'd rather have the pain done with."

"Are you sure that's wise?" he asked as she wrapped her arms around his middle and grasped hold of his backside.

"Yes." She pulled with remarkable force given her slight stature, and recognizing the determination in her eyes, he relented. With a single thrust, he broke through the barrier and sank deep into her core.

Pleasure jolted through him even as he heard her cry out in pain. He kissed her cheeks, her nose, her chin, but the rest of his body remained still until she nodded and wiggled her hips. "I'm ready."

He tested a stroke out and in and watched her expression

change, the pain replaced by desire. David thrust faster and deeper, her stilted breaths and eager hands inflaming his lust. Over and over he plunged. Each stroke more potent than the last, the urge for release came to a crest.

Her eyes closed and her pants for air became gasps of pleasure. He groaned as her pulsations around his length became too much. His muscles tensing, he pulled out just before he spilled his seed.

When he looked up, the beaming smile on Amelia's face lit the world like a sunrise after weeks of rain. "That was wonderful," she whispered.

"It was." Tenderness welled within him. Amelia amazed him in so many ways.

He grabbed his shirt and used his dagger to cut off a portion.

Amelia sat. "What are you doing?"

"You'll see." He dipped the fabric in the ocean and wrung it out, then returned to her side. "Lay back," he instructed.

She did as he asked, but her question hung in the air.

Carefully, he wiped the blood from her thighs. She made a soft sound, and he lifted his gaze to find her eyes glistening with tears. She didn't need to say anything for him to understand. It had been a long time since he, too, had felt a gentle touch and a caring hand.

While cleaning away the last of the blood, he spied a bruise on her hip. He brushed his hand over the spot. "What caused this?"

She propped herself up for a look. "I have no idea. Given the number of times I bump this or walk into that, I never remember what exactly causes each of my bruises." She pointed to her shin. "See? I have one there as well."

"You're a unique woman, Amelia."

She gave a chuckle. "Well said, and in a most cordial way, I might add." She lay back again, and he joined her, giving her his shoulder to rest her head upon.

Together, they stared at the heavens, the stars twinkling like jewels in the sky, and for the first time in God knew how long, contentment lulled him to sleep.

Chapter Eight

He had to escape.

David ran through the thick Madagascar forest. Fatigue slowed his pace. He wanted nothing more than to escape this godforsaken land.

Leaves rustled and a twig snapped, making his racing heart pound all the harder. He gripped his stolen lance tighter and crouched low in the brush. If they caught him, his master, the prince, would kill him this time, of that he had no doubt.

Footsteps. More than one set. A search party.

He waited, silent, hoping they would pass.

The sound of cautious steps grew closer. Too close. David readied himself. He would not go back.

The branch before him moved, swept aside by a hand. He thrust his lance forward and struck flesh and bone. A man screamed. Yanking the lance back, David turned and fled, glancing over his shoulder to determine how many would take up the chase. His feet slowed as dread burrowed its way into his chest.

A boy gaped down at the fallen man, his face filled with grief. Behind him a woman dropped to her knees. Her keening cries rang inside David's head as if the devastating sorrow was his own.

David startled awake and shivered despite the oppressive heat of day.

"Did you sleep well?" Amelia asked, her tone as cheerful as ever. Incredible and a little irritating, considering the boat rocked in short bursts from the choppy water, and gusts of hot wind rolled over them. Her lips had grown dry and rough, and her face was burned. Dressed only in her shift with her petticoats covering her legs, she held her gown over them both to shield them from the sun.

"Well enough," he answered, sitting up to hold one corner of their shelter aloft. He remembered what the Madagascar natives had said about dreams—that they were created by demons as a warning of what was to come. Would he make another woman cry as he had the day he'd escaped? He peered at Amelia as she studied the waves along the side of the boat and prayed the warning would never come true.

Handing him the rest of her gown, she rose to her knees, then crawled to the boat's edge.

"You're not thinking of taking a drink?" he asked, his own throat so parched it ached. "You'll make yourself sick."

"I won't," she assured him. "I'm just so warm." She scooped up a handful of water and splashed it onto her face.

Indeed, the day was the most uncomfortable so far, and Amelia had yet to utter a single complaint. "It's an awful tease, isn't it?" he asked.

She looked back at him, her face dripping. "What is?"

"To be so thirsty and completely surrounded by water you can't drink."

Amelia let loose a smile that stroked his heart. "I'd never thought about it that way," she confessed. She snatched up his discarded shirt and dunked it into the ocean, a gleam in her eye. "I think I'll wet myself down."

She wrung out the shirt, then patted her chest and neck with the damp material as she gazed out at the vast sea. The moisture made her skin gleam under the hot sun.

Amelia stiffened, and she inhaled a sharp breath.

"What is it?"

She pointed, and David watched a large, gray fin jut from the sea some ten feet away. The sight stopped his heart for a full beat. "Damn my soul."

The massive shark circled them in a wide arc.

"Sit back." David didn't wait for her to comply. He grabbed her about the waist and pulled her from the edge of the boat to sit next to him.

Amelia trembled, her attention fixed on the fin sinking into the sea.

"Don't worry. We'll be safe." He handed her the shirt she'd dropped. "Go ahead. You'll feel cooler."

She dabbed the wet cloth on her shift and exposed skin, all the while searching the water.

David moved to block her view. "Tell me your fondest memory."

"What? Why?"

"What we need is a distraction."

She looked around him. The fin submerged again as she watched, his shirt clutched to her chest. Clearly, she wasn't about to tell him her fondest memory.

"Very well, I'll tell you a story." Although the tales he had to share might be more disturbing than the shark.

. . .

They'd be safe here inside the boat. Nothing to worry about. They would not be eaten by a shark. The shark would not tip over their boat. She would not die of fright.

"Amelia, look at me." David grabbed her hand and gave it a squeeze. "You asked about why I became a pirate, about *The Wanderer*."

"You want to tell me now?" She searched the ocean for any sign of the shark, but David took her chin and steered her gaze back to him.

"Aye. Now." His intense stare bored into her, demanding her attention. "I told you that I escaped from the pirates who abducted me from my father's ship."

She nodded, her throat too thick with fear and thirst to speak.

"I hid from them on the coast of Madagascar, and once they gave up their search and sailed off, I waited for another ship to arrive, hoping they would take me home."

His soothing voice grounded her, relaxing her a bit, until from the corner of her eye she saw gray. The shark showed itself, closer this time, its immense body dwarfing the boat.

David saw it, too. He glanced toward the water despite his persistence in telling his tale. "As luck would have it, a tribe found me and took me to their prince. Once there, he made me his slave."

"A slave?"

Releasing her chin, he swallowed, and a muscle in his

jaw twitched. "I was a curiosity to him because of my pale skin. Most of the natives had never seen a white man before. The prince considered me a prize."

"Did he treat you well?"

"Reasonably well, if I did as I was told."

Indignation on his behalf burned through her. "If you didn't?" She sucked in a breath as the answer dawned. "Did he beat you?" David had that awful scar. Had it come from the prince?

"After I tried to escape," he frowned, and a spark of anger flared in his eyes, "he came at me with a knife and would have killed me if his brother hadn't convinced him to stop. He vowed to gut me like a fish if I ever attempted to escape again."

"But the next time you succeeded." A splash of water turned her attention to the sea, and he nudged her chin in his direction.

"Yes. The tribes frequently war with one another over cattle. Our village was attacked, and in the midst of the fighting, my guard became distracted, and I ran."

"How long—"

"Five months before an opportunity to escape arose. I managed to reach a port, and the crew of *The Wanderer* took me in," he said in a rush, his attention darting to the water.

The shark bumped the boat, and the craft lurched and bobbed. With a whimper, she clutched David's hand in a grip that should have crushed his fingers, as the shark disappeared beneath the surface.

"Blazes!" David picked up an oar and scanned the water. "We can't have him doing that again or he'll break us apart."

Break the boat apart? She panted for air. She couldn't

draw in enough breath. They were going to sink, or be eaten, or both!

David took one look at her and cringed. "Damn, I shouldn't have said that."

As the shark surfaced again and swam toward the boat, Amelia retrieved the other oar. "What should we do?" she asked, gathering her courage. Now was not the time to cower in fright.

"When it comes close again, we'll strike it with our oars."

Of course. Attack a shark, a beast longer than their rowboat. Made perfect sense. Her heart hammering in her ears, she readied herself.

The sleek, gray fish swiftly glided so close she could see its empty black eyes.

"Now!" David jabbed his oar forward, hitting the shark squarely in the snout before it could reach the boat.

Shaking, she swung her oar and smacked it on top of the beast's head.

"Aim for its eyes, gills, or nose," David shouted.

She began to pull the oar back when the shark flung its head to the side, ripping her weapon from her grasp and tossing it into the sea in one swipe.

"Bloody hell." David grabbed for the oar, but it floated out of reach as the shark submerged once more. "I need to go in after it."

"What? No. Leave it be."

"I can't. If we find land, we'll never make shore without both oars." He surveyed the ocean around them and eased himself into the water. "Distract the shark as best you can. Splash."

Make shore? What shore? "David! Come back." She

shivered, the icy fingers of dread clamping down on her shoulders. David swam quickly, taking care not to splash, his eyes darting all around.

She shifted to the other side of the boat and slapped the surface of the water, then wiggled her hands beneath. "Come here, shark." Good Lord, what was she saying? Even if her splashing worked, what would she do with the beast once it came? She'd best not worry about that now. She needed to keep the shark away from David.

Amelia glanced back as David grabbed the oar and changed direction. She swirled her arms in the water all the harder and smacked the surface until her palms stung. A streak of gray skimmed beneath the waterline not more than three feet from her. She bolted upright and snatched her hands away. Now what to do? She'd hit it with the remaining oar, but that might send the shark toward David.

On impulse, she snatched up her shoe and threw it as far as she could. What an odd thing to do. Did she think he was a dog who might go fetch? Even as the thought sprang to mind, the shark moved in the direction she'd thrown. Heavens. If he liked that, she had another. She picked up her other shoe and flung it another direction, well away from David, then turned toward the other side of the boat.

David had just reached the side, his face strained with exhaustion. He threw the oar she'd lost into the boat and began to hoist himself over the edge when the shark's large fin emerged close by. Too close.

"David! Faster," she screamed, grasping the remaining oar. Hysteria blurred her vision and spots of light flashed before her eyes. She shoved the oar toward the shark now nearly upon David. The end connected with its gills. It thrashed back and forth, knocking her paddle to the side, but she held on. She would not lose her grip this time. She jabbed again as David fell into the boat. Each smack of wood to flesh jolted through her, jarring her very bones.

Aiming for its small black eyes, she stabbed at the shark until it turned direction and swam away. It submerged beneath the water a fair distance off.

A mixture of anger and relief swamped her, the anger coming to the fore. She leaned over David lying on the bottom of the boat, panting for air. "Why would you put yourself in such danger?" she fairly shouted at him. "You could have been killed."

"We need both oars—"

"In case we find land," she finished for him. "So I've heard. The likelihood of which is minimal…" They were going to die out here… Her anger ebbed, replaced by despair. He wouldn't be in danger at all if it weren't for her. She should have forced him to remain behind. Her muscles turned to mush, and she sat down hard. "I'm sorry." He'd survived, and she should be thankful for that.

He closed his eyes and shook his head. "We are not going to die."

Water dampened her shift, soaking her legs. What? She scanned the hull and spied a crack in the wood. A sick feeling pooled in her stomach. She ripped a piece from her petticoat and tried to poke it into the leak. No use. Water still flowed. "We have a problem."

"I'm quite aware," he sighed. "Now that he's almost had a taste of me, he's sure to return. When he does, we'll both prod him along before he gets any ideas of attacking the boat."

"Not the shark. We have a leak." She pointed to the trickle.

Issuing a foul curse, he came closer and bent over the split. He retrieved his knife and used the tip to press the scrap of petticoat into the crack. "Hand me another."

She tore off a second piece and offered it to him. While he worked to wedge the cloth in, she studied the seas. A fin rose, but the shark kept its distance. Thank heaven. She scooped up water with cupped hands and threw it overboard. Not good enough. She grabbed David's shirt and dunked it into the spill, wringing it out over the side.

David sat on his heels. The leak had only become larger from his attempts. "Damn it to hell."

He searched beneath her petticoats and found the bowl he'd brought, then joined her in bailing out the boat.

Amelia held back useless tears as exhaustion settled in, the lack of food and water taking their toll. Her arms ached with each twist of David's shirt and her limbs grew heavy. No matter. She couldn't afford to succumb to self-pity. Ever watchful for the shark, she forced her body to move.

• • •

A streak of lightning lit the night sky. David could deny it no longer. They were going to die. Though the shark had left, the seas had grown restless, and the wind was beginning to howl.

His arms now as heavy as anchors tethered to his shoulders, he continued to bail out the boat. Across from him, Amelia wrung the shirt in her hands for the thousandth time, her movements slow and weary. Yet she didn't stop.

The fragile woman he'd worried about displayed a strength few men possessed.

Despite their efforts, the water level steadily rose. The battle would soon be lost.

Amelia raised a red, blistered hand to her forehead with a long exhale. Thunder cracked in the distance, and she flinched, glancing over her shoulder at the coming storm.

David forced a grin. "At least if it rains, we'll have something to drink." The humid air teased with the elusive taste of water, and thunder echoed around them. The storm had to be a few miles off.

She picked up the shirt once again, sopping up water from the leak, then tipped her head to the side. "Do you hear that?"

"What?"

"The sound is like thunder, but repeats at steady intervals."

David stilled and focused on the rumbling. The soft crashes had a rhythm. Inhaling deeply, he caught a whiff of loamy scent. He locked eyes with Amelia. "God love us. It's the surf hitting land."

Her glassy eyes crinkled at the corners, and a relieved smile touched her lips. Her hands kept moving, although she listed against the side of the boat. The look on her face was pure exhaustion.

He grabbed the oars and rowed toward the sound, the very thought of land invigorating his weary limbs.

Lightning snapped overhead, and the sizzle raised the hairs on his arms. Amelia hunched forward, still bailing water to keep the craft afloat.

David gripped the oars tighter. "We're going to make land before this storm hits us," he promised, his blood surging.

The surf grew louder. He glanced over his shoulder. A flash of lightning revealed a long island and trees standing tall. With ragged gasps, he rowed harder. Waves tossed the boat like a toy as he focused on the surf and the dry land beyond.

The ocean became a light blue as they reached the shallows, the sand below the surface almost white. Shadows of fish and plants spotted the sea floor. A number of them could be poisonous. "Stay inside the boat."

He didn't have to tell her twice. Amelia sagged against the side, her head lolled back, and her eyes closed.

He dragged his limbs over the side and hopped into the shallow water, nearly landing on his arse. The world spun, and his legs wobbled beneath him. His energy expended, he gripped the boat and caught his breath as the first droplets fell from the sky. Tipping his head, he opened his mouth. Rain dripped down his cheeks and spattered his brow. The fresh water was heaven on his parched throat. Thunder boomed. He forced his legs to move, and hauled the boat to shore. "Amelia, we're here." One last yank and he ran the craft aground. "And you thought you weren't lucky."

Her eyes opened a crack. With a groan, she attempted to climb out. She trembled, and David reached out an arm to assist her just as her legs buckled. "Hey, now." He caught her and lifted her limp body into his arms. Her head rested against his neck as he carried her toward the trees, her forehead feverish. He set her on the sand beneath the shelter of the trees and touched her heated cheek. "Amelia, open your eyes for me."

She didn't stir. A knot formed in his stomach that had nothing to do with hunger. She'd been without water for too long.

The wind whistled through the foliage, and the shower turned into a deluge. He cupped his hands to catch the rainwater. They shook so hard, he couldn't retain even the smallest amount. He raced to the boat on unsteady legs. Twice he fell, but he didn't slow his pace. Inside the boat, he found the bowl, then hurried back.

A stream of water ran off a large palm frond. He swallowed a mouthful, and filled the dish.

Soaked through, he sank to his knees beside Amelia and set the water aside. He positioned his arm under her shoulders and swept the hair from her face before lifting the water to her mouth. "Drink, Amelia." Still nothing. The beginnings of a headache throbbed behind his temples. He ignored it. "Amelia, drink some water."

He wet his finger and dragged it across her dry lips, lips that should be soft and smooth, as they had been when he'd first kissed her. David muttered a foul curse. He'd heard stories of what happened to men whose ships ran out of water at sea. Fever and delirium, followed by death. Was it too late to save her? She'd suffered so much since she'd been exiled from the ship. With never a complaint. Only unflagging courage.

David dipped his finger into the bowl and dribbled a few drops into her mouth. A low moan rose from her throat, and her head rolled to the side.

"That's it. Come back to me." He gave her another small taste.

She swallowed, her lips closing around his fingertip, and hope flared bright.

"Let's try this again." He picked up the bowl.

When the rim touched her mouth, her eyes fluttered open, and she took a sip.

He released a long breath. "Good girl. Take another."

Her eyes widened to the size of guineas, and she swallowed again, greedier this time. She lifted her hands to the bowl, clenching the sides and tilting it skyward.

"Not so much at first," he warned, pulling the bowl from her hands. "Sip."

Nodding, she slowly drank the rest of the water.

By the time she'd finished, bone-numbing fatigue settled into his shoulders and back. His muscles burned as he moved the empty bowl into the pouring rain to refill. His energy depleted, he lowered himself to the sand next to Amelia and cradled her head in the crook of his arm. They stayed beneath the trees as the storm raged. Water poured from the sky, battering the leaves above with a constant thrum.

As soon as the bowl refilled, David attempted to get Amelia to drink, with little success. She'd fallen back into an unconscious state. He swallowed some of the water, careful to take slow, measured sips, and moistened her lips again, dripping small amounts into her mouth.

She shivered, and he nestled her closer against him.

"Hold on, Amelia," he rasped and dropped a kiss to her forehead. "Hold on."

Chapter Nine

David tried to relax his muscles, careful not to jar Amelia as she rested in the crook of his arm. He needed sleep. Not that he'd give himself the luxury, not with Amelia burning with fever. Instead, he strained to stay awake, his very skin too tight for comfort.

He focused on the foliage above them and chewed another piece of coconut, the only nourishment he could find nearby. The slightly sweet flavor didn't appeal, but perhaps he would eventually grow to like the taste. Doubtful, but possible.

The rain tapped against the leaves in a steady rhythm as it had since dawn. Now early afternoon, the gray skies masked the sun from view, giving the breeze a chance to cool the air to a bearable temperature. The sights and sounds did little to ease his mind. Amelia fared no better than she had last night, and he was at a loss. What more could he do?

She shifted her head on his shoulder, and her low moan

vibrated against his chest. He picked up his rain-dampened shirt and wet her face and arms again. Her skin scorched him with every brush of his hand. Damn it. Would it help or hurt to move her out into the rain?

The wet cloth didn't soothe her as it usually did. Amelia's arm flailed to the side, and her body jerked and writhed.

David hoisted himself up to kneel at her side, his every muscle aching with exhaustion. "Easy now." He stroked her hair from her face. The delicate skin of her cheeks was mottled a bright red. Bracing her with an arm beneath her neck, he lifted the bowl to her lips. "Drink for me, Amelia." If he could get her to drink enough water, maybe she would cool down. Although so far no matter how much he'd forced on her, she hadn't sweat a drop.

Her eyes fluttered open. "David?"

He stared at her for a long breath. His muddled brain needed time to confirm he wasn't dreaming. "Yes, I'm here."

As soon as she heard his voice, her eyes flashed with panic. She rose and gripped his forearms with surprising strength, spilling water from the bowl onto her shift. "I didn't mean to kill her. Or hurt anyone else."

What was this? The result of a nightmare? He set aside the water and took her into his arms. She gave off the heat of a well-stoked oven. Of course. Delirium from her fever. That's all that this was. Still, her words tore at his heart. He knew that kind of guilt well. "You've done nothing wrong," he assured her. Gritty sand coated his fingers as he rubbed a path along her spine. "You've nothing to feel sorry for."

She clung to him, although her grip weakened with each passing minute. "I'll find a place far away to keep them safe," she insisted, her voice muffled as she nestled into his chest.

"I won't hurt anyone else."

Her whimper cut him deep, and he hugged her all the closer. He could only assume she spoke of her supposed curse. "Don't worry. You're safe. Everyone is safe." He settled a kiss on the crown of her head. Damn his soul, she felt good in his arms, better than any woman he'd known before. A smile tugged at his lips. How he missed the way she marveled at the world, every detail a discovery to be savored. So eager to experience life to its fullest. He straightened his spine, his determination strong. He would have that woman back, once he made her well again.

One more kiss on her head, and he pulled away from her. "You need rest."

"No." She held on to him, a tortured look on her features.

"Easy now. I'm here." He laid her back onto her sandy bed and lifted the bowl into place. "Now drink."

Her grip on his arm didn't loosen as she sipped from the cup, her eyes glassy pools. She peered up at him with unconditional faith. That look, so honest and trusting, buoyed his strength. He wouldn't let her die.

When it appeared she would stop, he tilted the cup higher. "More if you can."

With a feeble nod, she finished the water, her gaze wandering all about them. Although her eyes seemed unfocused, they were open at last.

Setting the bowl beneath the constant drip of a palm frond, he inhaled his first true breath since her fever had begun, taking in air that smelled clean and fresh. "How do you feel?"

"It's still raining."

Not the answer he sought, but he'd gladly take that over

the terror she'd shown before. "Here. Eat something." He raised a small slice of coconut to her lips.

She wrinkled her nose and swatted it away. At least she was responsive. He would assume it was a good sign. He tried again. "Come on now. It's coconut."

This time she accepted the offering, chewing slowly.

Plunging his palms into the rain, he dampened his hands, then smoothed the water over her legs as he had countless times already, the silky length of calf and thigh teasing his skin. He lifted a palm frond and waved it over her exposed legs in the hopes that the rapid evaporation would cool her faster. Amelia watched his ministrations closely, her face calm and relaxed. He moved his hands beneath the rain, ready to repeat the process when she crooked a finger and motioned him closer.

What could she…? He bent over her, and she motioned him closer still.

He moved his face to within inches of hers, and she used that same finger to press against his cheek, turning his head to the side. She lifted herself so that her mouth nearly touched his ear. "I like you," she confided, her whisper stroking his ear's outer ridge with the same devastating effect as a flick of her tongue.

A laugh tickled his throat as he pulled away. "I like you, too."

She closed her eyes and rolled her head, stretching her long, graceful neck. "You make me feel good."

Tenderness swept through him. She made him feel good, too. He ignored the purr in her voice and lifted the half-filled bowl to her mouth. "Let's try this again."

Eying him over the cup, she drank it all without prompting

this time. Excellent.

She placed her hand over his when he would have withdrawn the bowl, her fingers caressing, squeezing, inviting. He extricated his hand and picked up another piece of coconut meat. "Here. Have another."

Amelia ignored the offer. She reached out and ran a hand down his abdomen, sweeping over a spot just above his breeches. He flinched and sucked in a harsh breath, and she smiled, her lips bowing in a sensual curve. Bloody hell. What was she about?

"You're ticklish." She raised her hand toward his face. "You have pretty eyes… And I like your mouth," she added, her finger heading toward his lips but poking his cheek instead.

He made a move to catch her hand, but she snaked her arm around his neck.

"You have soft lips." Her arm tightened as she tried to pull him toward her, her luscious mouth puckered and ready.

A grudging laugh shook his shoulders. "Wait." He grasped her arm. "What's gotten into you?"

She blinked her eyes open, disappointment putting a pouting frown on her face. "But I want to kiss you."

Kiss him? Given different circumstances, he might oblige her. But not now. She wasn't herself. This was nonsense. "Rest. You're very ill."

She swept her hand along his cheek, her eyes pleading. "You can make me feel better."

He resisted the urge to nuzzle her hand. Instead, he drew it from his face and placed it on her stomach. She would be sleeping again soon, so he'd best keep his mind on task. He wrung out his dripping shirt and wiped it along her brow. A slight breeze ruffled her damp hair and an errant lock played with his fingers.

Skimming the cloth down one side of her face, he trailed his hand over her heated skin, so smooth and soft. She shivered and rolled her lower lip between her teeth, her gaze dropping to stare boldly at his chest. "When you touch me…" She stopped and swallowed. "When you touch me, I feel… tingly."

Her confession, although made in the throes of delirium, penetrated his senses, making him feel things he had no business feeling. He pushed all untoward thoughts from his mind and turned back to his task, running the damp shirt down her lean, shapely arms, one and then the other.

Her hand returned to his cheek. "Do you like touching me?"

He tensed. What a question. Her fever had gone straight to her head.

"Kiss me." Amelia tugged on his neck, but didn't wait for him to comply. She rose up and captured his lips with hers.

Dear God. The initial shock of it quickly melted, and relief took its place. She was awake and alive. The thought of Amelia slipping away, of losing her… He clasped her closer to him, letting the taste of her mouth and the brush of her tongue cure his aching body and soul. He worshipped her mouth with all the tenderness he felt inside. He used no finesse, not this time. His need ran deeper than that. It welled from a place he couldn't control and didn't fully understand. All he knew was how blessedly good she felt against him. His muscles trembled as the tension he'd held inside all day drained from him and soaked into the sand.

She broke their kiss with a radiant smile. "Oh, David. I love you."

Love? He peered into her eyes, eyes bright with fever, and his heart kicked his ribs with the force of a braying jackass. What the hell was he doing? What kind of man... He removed her arms from around his neck and laid her back onto the sand. "Amelia, I'm sorry...I shouldn't have—"

"You did nothing wrong." Her eyelids sagged shut, and her head lolled to the side. "Nothing wrong," she breathed dreamily.

Giving a low grumbling groan, he kneaded his forehead until he'd surely rubbed away two inches of his hair. Did Amelia really love him? No, she couldn't have meant those words. A fever made people say things... Burn his soul. He wasn't worthy of her and likely never would be.

His father had always told him he was a poor excuse of a man. A bitter taste filled his mouth as he remembered his time in Madagascar, the things he had done as a slave and what had happened when he escaped. Growing up, he'd thought that his father was wrong in his judgment, but now...

He sank to the ground and lay on the sand next to Amelia, studying her face as she slept. Her complexion had lightened to a rosy hue, and a slight sheen of sweat glistened on her forehead. At long last, she was on the mend. Next he would protect her heart.

• • •

How she hated snakes. Amelia lay stock-still on her belly after a dream-filled slumber, her attention riveted to the brown serpent an arm's length away. Vacant beady eyes fixed on her face, and a forked tongue flicked from its mouth. She shrank back, a tremor of revulsion rippling over her skin.

"David?" she called out, her voice a hoarse whisper.

The snake hissed in reply, and her next breath froze in her lungs. She tried to push herself up, but her arms were too weak to hold her.

"Ah, I see breakfast has arrived." David's boot pinned the snake to the ground.

Amelia startled, her heart clamoring for a way out. Where had he come from? She hadn't heard him approach.

Using his knife, he severed the snake's head from its body, and her insides churned. They weren't going to eat it, were they? "If that's what we're having for breakfast, I'll just have tea. Thank you." Then again, now that she'd satisfied some of her thirst, her hunger had returned, her stomach aching.

He glanced her way. "I haven't found much food as of yet. We have to make use of whatever we find." Tossing the head into the forest, he grasped the creature's body and lifted it from the ground. Its long length dangled from his hand.

Snake. She shuddered. Not something she'd ever thought she'd eat, but if it could fill her belly and restore her strength…

David gave her a weary smile. "I doubt you want to eat it raw. So, I'll set it over here until I can get a fire started." He walked a fair distance away and dropped the creature onto the sand.

She thought to call him back. What if there was another snake nearby? She scanned the grasses. Nothing. Not yet, anyway. Amelia rolled to her side and pushed off the ground, attempting to sit. Her arms shook and threatened to collapse when strong hands grabbed her, lifting her to her knees.

Relief and something else more feminine flooded

through her. She held on to David's shoulders to steady herself as she worked her legs out from beneath her, her fingertips sinking into warm skin and solid muscle. A vague recollection sprang forth—David hugging her so close, he had trembled, as if he couldn't bear to let her go. Without meaning to, she leaned in to the real man, desperate to feel his arms around her. She stopped as more hazy snippets of the memory flooded her mind. *Oh, sweet heaven.* Her pulse hammered an extra beat, and her face flamed. The things she'd said, the blissful kiss they'd shared. It couldn't be real. She would never say such things, do such things… No, it had to have been a dream. A silly, nonsensical dream.

"Are you ill? Is the fever returning?" David pressed his hand to her forehead. "You're cheeks look a bit red."

"The fever is gone, I'm sure," she insisted in a rush. *Dear God.* His touch in her dream seemed as real as the one she felt now. Images, sounds, and sensations surged forward. His hands on her skin, his lips pressed to hers in a bone-melting kiss that had blazed through her body to singe the very ends of her hair. She almost reared away from his hand, but his anxious concern stilled her.

He checked one spot, then another, sliding his hand along her forehead and moving to the sides of her face. "You're right. No fever." He expelled a breath and sat back. "How do you feel?"

"Tired." Avoiding his gaze, she relaxed against a tree trunk, mortified beyond compare. She struggled to remember what exactly had happened and what she'd said.

The morning sun glared off the beach, making her eyes burn and her head ache. She shielded her face and caught sight of several brown hairy cups resting near the bowl they'd brought, many filled to the brim with clear liquid. She reached out a trembling hand and picked one up, bringing it to her nose. A slightly sweet smell.

"Go ahead. Take a drink," David said. "You could probably use another."

She did look up then. Shadows darkened the skin beneath his eyes, attesting to the hardships he'd endured. He looked tired and drawn.

She sipped from the strange cup. The warm sweet water soothed her throat even as the coarse hair on the bowl scratched her lip. "Is this a coconut?"

"Yes. They won't be enough to sustain us, but they're better than nothing." Crouched beside her, he took up another coconut half and wedged his knife between the shell and the white inside, chipping off a piece. "Here."

He handed her the scrap. Their fingers touched, and another flash of clarity stole her vision. David had grazed his finger along her face, the stroke a loving caress. He'd looked at her in a way that was…adoring, like he couldn't live without her. That look had made her feel so good. Cherished. Desired. Happier than ever before.

The memory cleared, and she found herself staring up at David. He stared back, the expression on his face questioning and something else… Was that wariness? "Is something wrong?" he asked.

"I've heard of coconuts, but never actually seen one," she replied offhandedly even as she studied him harder. His intense brown eyes revealed nothing. Still, if what she remembered was real, then did he hold true affection for her? The thought turned her insides to warm honey.

He crooked one brow. "Other than since we arrived, you

mean."

"No, why would you say that?"

His eyes widened a fraction of an inch. "You've been drinking from these shells whenever the bowl has been empty. Don't you remember the last day and a half?" He sounded almost hopeful. Was he holding his breath?

"Not well." Of all she did remember, whether she drank from coconuts was not at the forefront of her mind.

In a subtle shift of muscle, he visibly relaxed. He lifted a hand to rub his mouth, yet a corner of his smile peeked through.

"What?"

"Nothing." He lowered his hand, and the smile was gone. "I came across some flint not too far from here." He stood and picked up a dark rock. "I'd best get to building a fire so we can put more food in your belly."

Relief. Obviously, he was filled with it. But why? Because of the kiss? Or perhaps because he'd shown his true feelings when he'd thought she wouldn't remember. If that were the case, should she let the matter lie?

David disappeared into the dense foliage where tropical forest met powdery white sand, and returned with twigs and dry leaves, creating a small pile. She chewed on another piece of coconut, one of many David had left for her, and contemplated the face she'd come to know so well. A dark stubbly beard shadowed his jaw, and his lean cheeks looked haggard from exhaustion. They'd grown closer since they'd left *The Wanderer*. In a strange way, she cherished that time with him. On the rowboat, she'd allowed herself those things she'd craved for the longest time—intimacy and affection. Maybe he had done the same. Now they were stranded here alone for God knew how long. Didn't they owe it to themselves to explore where their feelings lay?

"Was I awake at all yesterday?" she asked, the question tumbling out before she could stop herself.

Stacking larger branches to the side, he glanced in her direction. "I wouldn't say awake, not entirely."

She bit into another chunk of coconut and chewed furiously, determined to go on. "Were my eyes open?"

"For a time," he admitted as he knelt in the sand and assembled his tinder.

Another moment from the prior day wiggled itself free, and she choked on the bits of coconut she'd just swallowed. *Do you like touching me?* In her voice. Her voice. She coughed a time or two and cleared her throat, her stomach shrinking to the size of pea. "Did I say or do anything unusual?"

Silence reigned heavy in the air.

She peered at David. He didn't have to speak. His eyes said it all. They smoldered with a memory she only vaguely recalled. "Oh, dear God," she breathed, letting her head drop to her palms.

"Nothing much happened," David insisted.

When you touch me, I feel…tingly. She groaned. "The things I said." How much more had she forgotten? If she could, she'd dig a hole right here in the sand and bury herself. Or maybe not. Her jumbled dream spit out one more hint, one more hazy recollection. "Then you…" She looked up.

"Yes, we shared a kiss." David nodded, regret evident in every line of his body. "I'm sorry. I shouldn't have allowed it to happen."

Amelia concentrated, struggled to confirm her suspicion. She was fairly sure. The words echoed in her mind. Yes, those words had been spoken. "You… You said you loved me."

David sat up straight. "I what?"

She almost grinned. Poor man didn't think she'd remember. Which is probably why he'd been so relieved before. "Don't worry. If you're not ready to admit—"

"I didn't…" He struck the blade of his knife with the flint, and a spark flew into the air. "It was *you* who said the words."

She'd said them? Her heart sank to her navel, and tears sprang to her eyes. How silly. Of course she'd said them. With a jerk of her arm, she brought the crude cup to her lips again, rapping the hard shell on her teeth. She drank heartily, as if a sudden thirst had overcome her.

How could she have thought even for an instant that David would declare his love?

Just one look at him revealed the truth. Beads of sweat dotted his brow, and he only spared a glance her way before studying the rock in his hand.

Sadly, the water in her coconut was long gone before the need to weep, her emotions hanging on a precarious thread, most likely because of her recent illness. Yes, that had to be the cause.

"You were ill…out of your mind with delirium." David struck the steel again, closer to the tinder this time, then frowned. "I assumed you didn't mean what you said." His brow creased with concern, or possibly fear. "You didn't mean it, did you?"

She blinked her tears away. "I don't even remember saying the words."

David studied her as if he wasn't sure he should believe her. As if he waited for any bruises to show. She presented the relieved smile that belonged on her face. "How embarrassing. Let's not speak of it again." After all, she had no right to be distressed or heartsore. She didn't love him. He was right. She'd told him that in a moment of weakness, and any affinity they shared from their time at sea…had been inspired by the assumption that they were going to die.

Now that they'd survived being adrift, who was to say they wouldn't find a way off this island? Back on the pirate ship, she'd wanted to spare David from her misfortunes. Now was no different.

They would part ways for his own good. He would be safer without her.

Chapter Ten

The flash of disappointment in Amelia's eyes put a weight in David's stomach the heft of a coconut. Although she wouldn't admit it, she'd hoped he'd been the one to say *I love you*. Why? He wasn't worthy of her. Couldn't she see that?

She dusted the sand from her shift, sand that had been there this entire time. "Give me something to do. I'm feeling useless," she insisted.

David heaved a sigh. She should rest. She needed to recover. Yet he didn't blame her for wanting to keep herself occupied. A blush still stained her cheeks, and her fingers trembled as they straightened the linen.

"Very well. I've gathered some vines. You can knot them together for a fishing net." He hadn't seen many fish so far, but he had hope.

He rose, and his head swam for a matter of seconds. While he'd drunk his fill of rainwater, they'd need more than that and coconuts to survive. He handed her a snarl of vines and returned to his mound of tinder.

She immediately went to work. "Thank you for everything you've done for me. I realize yesterday must have been difficult caring for me and—"

"Don't worry yourself. It was nothing," he assured her, the quaver in her voice almost too much to bear. He attempted to light the leaves again. The spark didn't take hold. "I'm just glad you're feeling better." In fact... "You were *lucky* to survive." He waited for the coming argument. She had yet to admit to any good luck, no matter how obvious it was to him.

Amelia contemplated the vines in her hands. "True. We were both very fortunate to find land."

Had he heard her correctly? "You admit it?"

"How can I not?" She shrugged. "I thought we would die on that boat. I was sure of it."

Good. About time she came to her senses. He sat back on his heels and rearranged the dried palm fronds to better block the slight breeze.

"Of course that bit of luck doesn't excuse my poor choice of traveling across the ocean."

He dropped his hands to his knees and uttered a low curse. "You're still blaming yourself for our predicament?" Then again, why would he think otherwise? She'd been stubborn in her belief that she was some sort of harbinger of misfortune from the first moment he'd met her.

Her lips curled, a look of disgust on her face. "If it's not bad luck that puts me and others into harm's way, it's my foolish choices."

Although Amelia said the words, David had a feeling he knew who put them there. "Is that what your stepmother told you?"

Her hands tugged a bit harder on the vines. Her stepmother probably wasn't her favorite topic of conversation. Still, he couldn't stay silent. Not on this. Not after hearing her berate herself time and time again. "How old were you?"

She cast a suspicious glance his way.

Likely she worried he'd try again to talk her out of her silly beliefs. She was right to worry. "How old were you when your stepmother first came into your life?"

"Four or five. Why?"

What sort of woman would be so cruel to a young child? He smacked the flint to his blade with more force than needed. The spark caught, and a ribbon of smoke curled above the dry grass. He bent low and blew on the kindling. The smoke dissipated, and he sat back with a growl. "She sounds like a bitter woman. Perhaps even jealous... Did you have a good relationship with your father?"

Her hands stilled, and she hesitated so long, he thought she might not answer.

"My father is a patient, loving man. Even when I was at my worst, he showed me nothing but compassion."

There was a sadness to her tone he couldn't ignore. "At your worst?"

"I was an unruly child."

"In what way?" David tried his luck again, and once more smoke rose from the grass. He lightly blew on the spot, and a flame flared to life. He added more fuel to the fire. They might have snake for breakfast yet.

She released a laugh laced with self-reproof. "In just about any way imaginable. I had horrible tantrums. I constantly argued and talked back to my father." Her shoulders drooped as she plucked at the vines without much progress. "If he told me not to do something, I went out of my way to see it done."

How easy it was for her to speak of her own faults. Too easy.

"My father spoiled me," she continued, "but I also had immense anger."

"Anger?"

She frowned, her face crestfallen. "My father would tell me about my mother—how pretty she was, how smart and playful. I suppose I was angry that I would never get to know her as my father had." She shook her head. "My poor father endured a great deal. He grew desperate, and assumed I needed a woman in my life, so he remarried."

By the time he looked back at the fire, the flame had died low. He added more kindling and a few sticks until it grew to a small crackling blaze. "Did his marriage improve your temperament?" He doubted it would, not with a termagant for a stepmother.

"My behavior grew worse for a time, but eventually…"

How badly they must have got on. "Did she discipline you?"

"She tried. No supper, early bed, locked in the attic for the better part of a day… She even punished me with a switch." A whisper of resentment tainted her voice for an instant. As well it should.

"She hit you?" he asked, louder than he'd intended.

"Not for long. It galled her that in the midst of the punishment I would laugh in her face."

"I find that hard to imagine. You're such a sweet soul." He'd never so much as glimpsed a hint of temper from her. "Did she give up?"

"No." Amelia closed her eyes and released a breath

before opening them again. "She pointed out the obvious. That I had no right to act the way I did because..." Her voice broke as if she were choking on the words. "She told me that I'd killed my mother, that my mother had died giving birth to me." Her chin trembled, and she raised a hand to her lips. "I hadn't known. My father never said."

The bitch. What a shock that must have been for a young child. David stepped closer, eager to hold her, to comfort her.

Amelia held up a hand and looked away as if to tell him she didn't need coddling. "From then on, I vowed to be good...for my father. I could finally see how miserable he was because of me. Not only had my mother perished bringing me into this world, but he'd married a shrew because I was a terrible child."

What? David clenched and flexed his hands, outrage silencing him for a full minute. How could she be so damned accepting? It galled him to think... "For the love of Christ! Your hag of a stepmother tells you that you're responsible for your mother's death, and you accept it as fact?"

Her spine straightened. "I think I always knew I was at fault. I just didn't want to believe it." She cleared her throat. "Not long after, my father fell off his horse and injured his back—"

"And your stepmother decided that, too, was your fault." He could see it clearly now. Once her stepmother had realized how well her first lie had worked, she'd used that ploy again and again.

Amelia's stare turned cold. "Yes, she was convinced I had something to do with his accident. She told me if I loved him, I would stay away. But—"

"Did you stay away?"

"Initially, no. Not until he suffered a second injury when I slipped into his room to see him." Her movements stiff, she yanked on the vines as if that would somehow loosen the knots instead of tighten them. "I didn't want to believe my stepmother, but she was so unrelenting, and the accidents happened far too often."

"What of your stepsister? Did your stepmother drive you from her, too?"

Her silence bedeviled him. "Don't you see what she's done?" he asked, incredulous beyond compare. "She uses lies and your love for your family to manipulate you into distancing yourself from your father and stepsister."

"I need to keep them safe," Amelia snapped.

"Nonsense. This isn't about protecting your family." He took a guess, a theory that had formed in his mind the moment he'd heard how her mother had died. "This is about punishing yourself."

Blue-green eyes flared wide, a mixture of shock and pain in their depths.

"It's as if you're banishing yourself from those who love you to somehow atone for your sins. No doubt that's the reason you never show anger, frustration, or resentment— because you're too busy focusing those emotions on yourself."

She gripped the vines in her hands, her knuckles turning white. "My father's life was ruined because of me. Both my parents suffered because of me."

Damn her vindictive stepmother and the lies she'd spewed. "Your mother's death wasn't your fault, and I'm sure she wouldn't want you to carry this guilt. As for your father marrying a bitch, he did that of his own free will."

"Stop!" She threw the vines in his direction, her frustration evident in her every movement. "You don't know what you speak of."

He held back a surprised laugh at her first real show of ire. A good sign, to his way of thinking. He'd best push on. "You're not keeping anyone safe. You're running away."

"My family is better off without me." Despite her weakened state, she rose unsteadily to her feet, her will strong.

"Are they?" He stepped closer, ready to grab her should she fall. "Do you think they're happy now with you halfway across the world?" He moved closer still, the urge to touch her flushed cheek and smooth aside the errant lock of hair that partly masked one eye almost too tempting to resist. "I seem to remember you saying that your stepsister fell down the stairs in her hurry to greet you after you'd left home following an argument. Another instance of running away, I might add."

Her eyes lowered to the sand, and her brow wrinkled.

"At any time, did your father or your stepsister ever tell you to keep your distance from them? Or was it always your stepmother who warned you off?"

All frustration drained from her features, replaced by confusion. "They should have. You've seen what can happen."

"Yes, we've run into some bad luck, but we've had good luck, too."

She worried her lip, her shoulders drooping.

He encircled her waist with an arm. The force of her anger gone, she sagged against him.

"Stop listening to the shrew," he quietly pressed. "Purge her from your head. You, your father, your stepsister, all deserve to be happy, together."

She raised her eyes to his, doubt still clouding them.

Cradling her head in his hands, he stared deeply into those eyes, determined to see that doubt fade. "You are an amazing woman. Strong, kind, and compassionate. You deserve happiness… Say it."

"What?"

"Say, 'I deserve to be happy.'"

Amelia's lips tilted in the slightest of smiles. "I deserve to be happy."

Not good enough. "Louder. I want to hear you shout."

Her smile grew into a genuine grin. "I deserve to be happy!"

"And my stepmother is a vindictive bitch."

David laughed outright at her look of shock. "Very well. You don't have to say that. Just believe it." Gazing at her smiling face, he was sorely tempted to lower his lips to hers and kiss her worries away. But he shouldn't, and he wouldn't. She needed to return to her family, to start anew. And she needed to do it without him dragging her down into his muck.

"I don't suppose you know how to dress and cook snake," he asked as he released her and urged her to sit.

"Afraid not."

He retrieved the vines for her, then headed back to his pile of kindling, the flame long gone. As he bent to relight the tinder, he couldn't help himself. He glanced at Amelia, the vines in her lap but her attention on the sea.

Since he'd met her, he'd found a purpose to his life, something that had saved him from drowning in his own bitterness. He admired her in so many ways. She'd come to mean more to him than he cared to admit, too much for his own good. It would be hard to let her go.

Chapter Eleven

Amelia scanned the grass around her. No snakes, at least not so far. She shivered anyway and slapped another mosquito determined to taste her blood as she followed David through the forest brush. Despite the occasional bite to her exposed skin, she was glad she only wore her shift in this damp, motionless air.

She should be looking for snakes as a source of food rather than out of wariness. After all, they'd eaten one for breakfast, although not very filling and rather tough to chew. She had yet to decide if so little food was really better than none at all. While in the rowboat adrift at sea, her stomach had grown used to being empty. Now it groaned and ached in complaint.

David looked back. "You didn't have to come with me," he repeated, having said the same several times over the last twenty odd minutes.

"I wanted to." She walked on, her legs already growing

tired. "I'm too thirsty to stay behind," she lied. She didn't want to be alone. She'd rather have David's company. "Besides, I'm feeling stronger." At least when compared to earlier in the day.

"You won't be able to drink the water until I boil it." He stopped and waited for her to catch up. "That is if we find some."

So tense and stern. Granted, they'd run out of water hours ago. Still, she teased, "Are you saying we'll never find water because I'm slowing you down too much?"

He cocked his head to the side and his mouth twitched at the corners. "No. I'm saying there may not be any to find."

She graced him with her biggest smile. "Good…because now that I'm here, you'll have to tolerate my intrusion the best you can."

That twitch of his lips turned into a lazy grin that made her tingle all over. "I'll try." He held out his hand and she took it, the press of his palm against hers putting her at ease.

She didn't know what she would do without him. To have him by her side through this ordeal was downright…lucky. She'd never thought she'd use that word to describe herself. But it was true, at least some of the time. David had been right in her reasons for leaving. Once he'd pointed out her need to punish herself, his logic made so much sense. She'd simply never thought of it that way before. His reasoning felt right, as if a huge weight had been lifted from her shoulders. Amelia tilted her head back and inhaled a deep breath.

The canopy of trees filtered most of the sun, the faint sparkle of light glorious. Palms, pines, and other trees she didn't recognize stood tall around them. She took in the sound of flapping wings overhead and the twitter of birds, the rich earthy scent of soil and plants. The world had righted itself in the course of a day.

Another trickle of sweat trailed between her breasts, and she slapped at an insect on her neck.

David's attention jerked to their left and he tugged her in that direction, urging her faster. "Look over there." He pointed to a clearing in the distance.

She didn't see the water until they were several paces closer. The sun glinted off the surface of a sizable blue pool. Magnificent. Another stroke of luck! She rushed forward, pulling David by the hand. Once at its edge, she stopped and gazed in wonder at its serene beauty, then dropped to her knees. She dipped her hands into the clear water. Warm and inviting. She wet down her arms. "How will we carry the water back to the shore?" She looked at the dense forest around them. "Or will we move our shelter here?"

David crouched beside her. "We'll move our shelter for easy access."

Her legs still wobbly, she shifted her balance and the dirt beneath her gave way. With a shriek, she tipped forward. David grasped her by the shoulders. Too late. Her momentum already carried her toward the water's surface. Only now it carried him too. To his credit, he didn't let go even when all was lost. They both tumbled into the pool.

The water was deeper than she would have imagined. When she resurfaced, she stood on tiptoe to keep her mouth above water. David had no such problems. His shoulders rose above the waterline. "Are you injured in any way?" he asked. His hands roamed over her limbs to make certain.

"No. I'm fine." She patted his hands away. Normally, she would have assumed this accident was her due, but she refused to look at it that way anymore. "I simply thought I would cool off with a swim."

He chuckled. "You did, did you?"

"Indeed." Perhaps a fib, but the water was soothing. "It's nice to finally have the salt rinsed from my skin."

"And it will keep the bugs at bay," he agreed, floating onto his back.

She'd never learned to swim. The fear of drowning in the attempt had been too much, what with her history of troubles. But with David so near, she felt no such qualms. She lifted her feet and flailed her arms, eventually sinking until she stood once more. She tried again. This time David watched with interest.

"No need to thrash," he told her. He walked over and moved her arms in a slower fashion, widening the strokes to encompass more area.

"I'll drown."

"Trust me. You won't." He lifted her legs out from under her, and she struggled to get free until he pulled her close, her side to his chest. "Our bodies are made to float without much effort. Let me show you. Lie flat."

He raised her level with the surface and attempted to release her.

"No!" She clasped hold of his shoulders, her heart pumping a wild beat. "Don't."

Staring deeply into her eyes, he vowed, "I won't let you sink. I promise."

She did trust him. David would keep his word. He glanced down at where she held him fast. Slowly she let her arms go slack, and he lifted her to lie on her back again. The water made odd muffled sounds in her ears, and the sun glared into her eyes.

"Slow your breaths. No need to worry. I won't let go until you're ready."

She might never be ready.

David looked down at her, his warm brown eyes filled with affection, and a reassuring smile swept across his lips. He seemed carefree and at peace with the world. It suited him.

She closed her eyes and relaxed her muscles one by one, trusting that David would keep her from sinking—until he let go. With a gasp, she struggled to float, her body arching and her legs rigid. No use. As soon as her face dipped below the surface, all reason fled and panic took hold.

David's arms returned, but not before she'd elbowed him in the shoulder, barely missing his chin. "Ho now. I've got you. You're safe," he said, bringing her close.

She latched onto him as tightly as a burr in his shirt, if he'd been wearing one. "You let go of me!"

"You were ready," he insisted.

"Hardly." She wrapped her legs around his waist for good measure.

"Well then, I'm sorry." He tried to peel her arms from his neck, but she wasn't about to let go. "Come now. Let's try again."

She shook her head, her face buried deep in the side of his throat. "No."

"I thought you liked to try new experiences."

The rumble of David's voice inches from her ear sent a tremor along her spine. Her cheeks flaming, she leaned away. Had he been referring to that day on the boat?

"Are you ready for another…go?"

She could tell the instant his thoughts veered in the same direction. His eyes became a molten brown, and something below the surface of the water elongated and hardened. And it wasn't a fish.

An intensity brightened his gaze and sharpened his features, but the sight of his lips drew her closer. Glistening from the water, his mouth beckoned. The taste of him in the boat had been salty and warm. What would he taste like now?

The first touch of her lips on his was tentative, but as soon as he kissed her back, she delved deeper, luxuriating in the feel of his tongue, in the intimacy they shared. She kissed him with all the tenderness and gratitude that had been building up inside, and his response, so unhurried yet passionate, carried her away from their hardships to a world more pleasant.

The deeper she slipped into this foreign land, the more eager she was to share herself with him. Her nerves buzzed to life, her skin becoming sensitive to the water that embraced them, the rub of his chest against hers, and the strength of his arms around her.

His hands roamed over the sides of her breasts, then lower to cup her backside while his mouth swept along her jaw to graze her throat. She rolled her head to the side, the sun warming her face. Her lower parts tingled as he pressed her hips closer, his arousal thick against her core.

He slipped his hand down her leg and beneath her shift. In a sensual slide of his palm, he brushed along her thigh and over one cheek, and the desire to touch him overruled all else. Securing one arm around his back, she moved the other to the waist of his breeches and reached inside. Smooth skin and a perfectly rounded behind. She nuzzled her hips closer and heard his sharp intake of air, followed by a groan.

David clasped her to him and waded to the shore, setting her on the soft grass. He lay beside her, propped up by one arm, his hand finding her breast through her wet shift.

More. She needed more. She needed to feel, not think. If she thought about what they were doing, she might come to her senses, and she didn't want to stop. This felt too good. Covering the hand on her breast, she ran her mouth over David's cheek to his ear. She traced its outline with her tongue and felt a tremor run through him. His hand molded over her breast, rubbing her nipple with his thumb. Each flick brought to life a flicker of heat that traveled from her chest to the juncture between her thighs. She panted for air, the sensations conjuring fantasies she'd best not imagine—David by her side now and forever. Together they'd be happy.

David's mouth and tongue replaced his thumb, and a hunger flared bright that had nothing to do with food. She swept her hands over the warm inviting skin of his shoulders and back, her fingers cherishing his scar as much as the smooth planes. At the waist of his breeches, she tugged the fabric lower, baring his pale hips and more. She didn't stop until his lower half was as exposed as the rest of him.

"*Mmm*. My turn," he growled as his fingers snagged the hem of her shift and lifted. Both hands glided up her body in a long, tantalizing caress that had her arching for more. David's smoldering gaze watched as the garment grazed her sensitive breasts, catching slightly on her nipples as if it, too, wanted to play. With an admiring smile, he drew the shift over her head and tossed it aside, then latched onto one nipple. Pleasure shot through her in a surprising jolt, and a groan rose from her throat.

She tipped her head back, her eyes heavenward. Coconuts. Three hung above them. *A coconut will not fall on our heads...* The thought vanished as quickly as it came, her aching need building with David's mouth suckling, his tongue licking. Eager to touch more of him, to feel *all* of him, Amelia reached low and clamped hold of his manhood. He flinched, sucking in a sharp breath, and she quickly released him.

"I'm sorry. Did I..."

"No," he assured her with a chuckle. "Feel free." He guided her hand back to his length.

Her fingers explored the soft skin from base to tip, the latter making his stomach muscles tense. Such a wonder. The contrast of rigid flesh and smooth skin. He moved his hand between her legs, the heady touch inspiring her to grasp hold of him again. One of his fingers penetrated her core. She moaned and held all the tighter. On the second plunge of his finger, he thrust his hips, his length rubbing over her palm. Oh my. Each stroke of his hand was more potent than the one before. "David, please."

He shifted his hips and slid his length inside her in a sensuous thrust that made her shiver. She wrapped her legs around him. He filled her so completely, as if the two of them were one.

She'd never felt so close to someone as she did with him. He stared at her with desire and devotion, and true happiness filled the void in her heart that had ached for so long. David withdrew and thrust into her again and again, his hooded eyes taking in her sighs and whimpers as the pleasure at her apex heightened to an unbearable peak. She cried out. Pulsations of ecstasy rippled through her.

He nuzzled her neck and plunged harder and faster until he pulled out of her with a shout of release, then collapsed to his back. She rested her head on his shoulder, strangely feeling no regrets. Later, she would ponder the rights and wrongs of it all, but for now she'd let herself be content.

They lay in the grass for the longest time, each deep in their own thoughts. She stayed silent, afraid to break the spell that bound them together, even knowing the moment would be a fleeting one.

Would they forever live on this island? Would she ever find her way home? And if they were somehow saved, what then? She was afraid to ask. This morning, he'd made it perfectly clear he didn't love her. So what was this? Desire, an escape from the hunger and thirst that plagued them? She released a long exhale. Enough thinking. Chances were good that they'd have plenty of time for that in the coming days, here alone together. "Shall we gather up some coconuts to carry water back with us? I'm rather thirsty."

David nodded. "As am I." He stood and helped her to her feet before donning his breeches. As she wrung out her shift, he gave her a distracted kiss, and she wondered if his thoughts ran along the same path as hers. Dressed again, she joined him in collecting coconuts scattered on the ground. They cracked the shells open and filled them with water. Once saddled with as many as they could carry, they set off.

The forest dimmed, the sun lower in the sky.

Amelia adjusted the four shells in her arms and glanced over at David. "You've been quiet."

He shook his head as if his silence were of no consequence. "So have you."

Once again, she contemplated what their future held. While they couldn't control whether they would be stranded here forever, they could decide to stay together no matter what happened. But how to begin? *Do you care for me? Did you make love to me solely because of lust or… Dear Lord. I can't be so bold as to say that.*

A bell chimed in the distance. Her pulse leaped. What on earth… Where was it coming from?

She exchanged a look of wonder with David as giddy exhilaration shot through her veins. A bell meant people. They could be rescued!

His face filled with hope, David turned toward the sound. He stood listening, then set his coconuts on the ground and peered up at the trees. Picking a sturdy trunk, he grabbed hold and began to climb.

"Be careful," she called as he rose higher and higher. Her throat constricted, growing tighter the farther he climbed. If he fell… She stepped back a few paces, as if that would somehow protect him from her curse. *No! I am not cursed.* She simply had to get used to the idea.

Near the top of the palm tree, David stopped and let out a whoop. "A ship," he shouted down to her. "It's sailing to an island not too far off."

Thank God! She jumped for the sheer joy of it and sloshed water all over the front of her shift. Her mind raced. How could they get the attention of the ship? A fire? Could they row to the vessel before it sailed away? But, their boat had a leak. It would have to be repaired before they could go anywhere.

"There's a light on the island, guiding the ship to shore," David yelled from his perch.

Which meant someone lived on that island, someone who had contact with the outside world. They were saved! Assuming they could fix their boat. Even so, excitement rippled through her, making her want to dance and sing…until she saw David's hold on the tree slip. She cried out and raced toward him as he slid several feet, then regained his grip.

"I'm fine," he assured her, descending to the bottom and hopping to the ground. Raw scrapes lined the inside of his arms and along one calf, but he gave them no heed. He looked up at the sky and the elation on his face dulled. "It'll be dark soon. We'll have to wait until tomorrow to find what I need to make pine pitch in order to seal the crack in our boat." David retrieved the coconuts he'd left on the ground. "In the meantime, we can quench our thirst. Come on. Let's go." He led the way the way back to the beach.

She followed, but all too soon her feet became sluggish and heavy.

"What's wrong?" he asked, slowing his pace.

Once they left this island, their time together would soon end. Unless… "If we find a way to the other island, will you be returning to London?" She desperately wanted to see her family again, to make things right with them. Perhaps she and David could go to England together.

"No, I have no intention of ever returning." A frown flickered. "Amelia, what happened between us at the pond… We shouldn't have—"

She held up a hand. She couldn't bear to hear him finish. "This has nothing to do with that," she lied.

"You deserve so much more," he finished anyway.

Yes, yes. He'd said that before. What rubbish. His sorry excuse stemmed from his father's criticism. "Why won't you go back to London?" she pressed.

David turned and marched on ahead. "My father wouldn't want me back."

"How can you say such a thing?" she asked as she trailed behind him. "He must have been incredibly relieved when you returned from Madagascar."

"I haven't been to London since I left on my father's ship."

"Oh, David." She could only imagine his family's worry, the despair that they might never see him again. "You must assure your family that you're safe. They may be searching for you."

"After a year? Not likely." His strides lengthened, and she had to hurry to catch up.

"Surely your father will be thankful to see you survived your capture no matter what stood between the two of you before. Besides, what of your brother and sisters? I am sure your family cares about you. You should—"

"The man they care about no longer exists. Who I am now…" They reached the shore, and David headed for the pile of ash left from their last fire. "It's better if they believe I'm dead."

How could he say such a thing? "Are you trying to punish your father?"

David didn't reply as he set down his coconuts and threw fresh kindling onto the ash.

She placed the coconuts she carried next to his. He could be so stubborn when he wanted to be. "Or are you punishing your family for not standing up to him on your behalf?" she needled.

"Fine." A muscle in his jaw flexed and tensed. "I'll send a letter. In fact, you can take it to them for me."

"A letter? That's hardly the same." Whether her objection

was solely for the benefit of his family or if it stemmed from the ache in her chest, she couldn't say. His suggestion that she ferry the letter… She would be going back to England without him and would likely never see him again. She swallowed the rising lump in her throat. "If not England, where will you go?"

He used his flint and dagger to spark a fire. "I suppose I could return to *The Wanderer*, if I ever find it again."

Return to the life of a pirate and a thief. The thought left a sour taste in her mouth. "You're better than those men you call brethren."

"Am I?"

"Yes. The simple fact that you didn't side with them when they cast me off attests to your honor."

He struck his blade with the flint again, the spark catching on the dry tinder and burning it away. "At least there I'm treated as an equal, as a man."

"If you face your father and tell him—"

"No. It isn't only the resentment toward my father that's keeping me from him." David rubbed a hand over his face and uttered a low curse.

She kneeled beside him and placed a hand on his arm. "Tell me."

Rich brown eyes filled with shame met hers.

"Please," she prompted. Whatever he was holding back was eating him up inside, that much she could sense.

"When I finally escaped the prince…" His voice hitched, and his gaze dropped to the sand.

"Go on."

"I worried that the guards would pursue me, and as I passed through a nearby forest, I heard footsteps, so I hid." His nostrils flared with his next breath and his jaw grew rigid once more. "The sound came closer and closer until it was upon me... I panicked and used my lance to run the man through." His eyes glistened, and his chin quivered. "I ran from the place, but when I looked back..."

His sadness brought a tear to her eye, and she wrapped her arms around him.

David held her in a desperate grip. "His wife and son saw it all. They mourned over his body. He wasn't a guard, just a man with his family, and I killed him." David's chest shook as he gasped for air.

"You couldn't have known." Amelia stroked his spine, her heart hurting with him.

"Tell that to the boy who lost his father."

"Oh, David."

He pulled away and wiped his cheeks with the back of one hand. "My father always told me what a worthless man I'd become. Little did he know—"

"No." She took his chin in her hand and directed his face toward her own. "Your father is wrong, and always has been. Since the day we met, you've been nothing but brave and thoughtful. Truth be told, you are the finest man I've ever known."

The pain in his features lifted a bit. "You have brightened my world in more ways than I can say. I'm very lucky to have met you." He cradled her head in his hands and stared deeply into her eyes. "Thank you. You've been a good friend, one I will sorely miss."

He hadn't changed his mind. He wouldn't be going to London. She could see it in his eyes. They would part as friends. They'd never promised each other more. It should be enough. But it wasn't, and it never would be.

Chapter Twelve

David sat in the sand before the brilliant sunrise. He drew his bow across the violin strings and reveled in the melody he played.

In the meadow by the stream
All our days spent in dreams
A joyful life for you and me
My true love, Guinevere

The music flowed from him even as his mind wandered. He should be collecting the pine pitch ingredients he'd need to repair the boat. Why he delayed remained a mystery.

A movement from their crude shelter caught his eye and a mussed beauty emerged from within. He brought the violin to his lap as the mystery revealed itself. To spend a few more moments with the lovely creature walking his way, he'd delay the repairs forever. She helped him remember the person he once was, the one who had enjoyed the beauty in life, the one who was carefree and happy. With Amelia near, glimmers of that man came through.

"Don't stop," she insisted once she'd nearly reached him.

He rose to his feet and brushed the sand from his backside. "I've already played so long my fingers have grown sore. Time to stop, for now."

As they strolled back to their shelter, she stared up at him, a curious look on her face. "You've shaved."

He rubbed a hand over his smooth jaw. For some reason, this morning had been the first time in a long while that he'd cared to take note of his appearance. "Do you like it?"

Her slight smile brightened her face almost as much as her rising blush. "I do."

Satisfaction swelled in his chest. "I have something for you."

"You do?"

He strode ahead toward their spent campfire where he'd left his prize. Once there, he picked up a spiny, green oblong ball the size of a small muskmelon and presented it to her like the finest gift. "It's a fruit called soursop. I've heard *The Wanderer's* crew speak of it."

Although his stomach had been eating a path to his spine since he'd found the fruit, Amelia's reaction was well worth the wait. Her eyes grew large, and a delighted smile graced her lips.

"Come. Let's eat." Planting himself on the ground, he patted the spot next to him, then used his knife to slice into the soursop, exposing white pulp with black seeds.

Amelia sat, and he handed her half. He took a bite and motioned for her to do the same.

She sank her teeth into the smooth white pulp and groaned. "Delicious."

Indeed. The fruit was sweet with a tart bite. They ate with relish, not wasting a morsel. Well, except for the seeds. He finished first and watched Amelia enjoy her meal.

A pretty blush pinkened her cheeks, and she paused, clearing her throat. "Tell me, where did you learn to play so well? You have great talent."

David bowed his head. He hadn't heard a compliment in so long he wasn't sure what to do with one anymore, so he focused instead on answering her question. "When I was a small boy, I saw an old man on the street play with such skill, I told my mother I wanted to learn, and she arranged lessons for me. She even bought me this violin."

"Your father had no issue with that?"

"He was a happier man then." How odd to remember. He'd almost forgotten those days. "My mother could have talked him into anything... He adored her." They all had.

"What was she like?"

He looked at Amelia again, her cheeks returning to their normal shade as she finished her fruit. "She was a lot like you...understanding and kind, friendly... She never met a person she didn't like. She could always find some admirable quality in everyone she came into contact with. Which I suppose explains how she ended up with my father." Her death had been the worst thing to happen to their family. For those first few months, his father had drunk to excess and hidden himself away. He'd barely looked at his children, especially David, the youngest, the one she'd been the closest to. "Maybe that's why he resented me."

"What do you mean?"

"My mother and I were inseparable for a time. We were very much alike." Perhaps too much. "After she died, my father changed, became irritable whenever I was near, as if he couldn't stand the sight of me." He shook his head. "It didn't take long before he decided my music lessons were a waste of time, before he began trying to change me into someone more like him."

"Maybe he didn't realize what he was doing. Maybe if you talk to him…"

No, he'd never been able to talk reason to his father. Why would now be any different? He rose to his feet. "I'm going to head to the pond. I saw some pine trees there, and I'll need sap to make pine pitch."

She set aside the fruit's skin, the meat all gone. "I'll go with you."

"There's no need."

"I want to," she insisted, her eyes hopeful.

How could he resist? He extended his hand to help her up, and they entered the forest. "Fine then. You can search for animal droppings on the way. I'll need them, too."

Her nose wrinkled, and he laughed. "Or I can look for them."

As they walked, a troubling thought occurred to him. One that should have surfaced the prior day. "I've been wondering about the ship I saw yesterday. What if it's a pirate ship? The pirate haven of New Providence can't be too far from here."

"Did you see a flag?"

"Not clearly," he admitted as he stepped through a combination of grass, sand, and soil. "I think it would be best if I rowed to the island on my own, looked around, and returned for you once I'm assured it's safe."

"You'd leave me here? Alone…with the snakes?"

He almost smiled at that. "You'll be fine."

"I'd rather go with you."

As he knew she would. He couldn't allow it. "Please don't argue with me on this. Not all pirates are the same. While some will respect a woman's virtue, many live by no rules and would just as soon have their fun."

Her lips pursed and twitched, but she said no more on the subject. Soon the freshwater pond came into view, and with it an unexpected sight that made his protective instincts flare to life.

Beside him, Amelia gasped.

A black man was crouched by the water, with a large gourd in one hand and another on the ground at his side. He wore only breeches, the dark skin of his chest marred in places by whip marks. His eyes wide, he appeared as startled to see them as they were by him.

David hurried to put himself between Amelia and the man. "Who are you?" David called out.

The stranger held his silence, his gaze darting about as if deciding whether to flee or stand his ground.

"Who are you?" David repeated.

Amelia grasped hold of David's arm. "Let him be. He's just getting water."

"Isaac," the man said as he rose to his full height with a look of challenge. "Your name?"

An old scar on Isaac's cheek captured David's attention. A burn. And the state of his breeches, all tattered and worn.

"David," he replied, as he took a step forward, his hand resting on the hilt of his dagger. "Do you live on this island?"

Isaac's brow furrowed as if he didn't understand.

"Where are you from?" he pressed.

Still no answer. What if... He repeated his last question

in a language he'd hoped to never use again, in Malagasy, the language of Madagascar. "*Avy aiza kay ianao?*"

Isaac's brows rose, but he didn't answer.

He searched for the words and spoke again. "*Azonao ve ilay tiako ho…tenenina?*" *Did you understand what I said?*

"*Eny.*" *Yes.*

Good. Although, if he understood, why hadn't he answered? Likely because he didn't want to say from where he'd come. Very well. "*Firy…*" *How many…* Bloody hell. He couldn't remember. "*Firy…*" Damn.

David sensed Amelia move behind him. From the corner of his eye, he watched her approach the pond's edge. She bent down and dipped her fingers into the water.

To hell with this. He gave up trying to recall the words. "Are there others here with you?"

"No." Isaac spoke with such vehemence, David couldn't help but wonder if the man was answering the question or expressing his frustration.

David glanced at the gourds the man held. They would have taken some time to dry before they could be of use. Of course, the man could have brought them here from somewhere else. He thought to ask how long Isaac had been on the island. Before he could, Isaac growled something in a language David had never heard before.

Amelia screamed. David turned in time to see her stumble backward and fall at the edge of the pond as an alligator emerged from the water. It lunged toward her.

He ran full out to where she lay, his heart pounding from his chest.

Fighting for breath, she scrambled away, but she wouldn't be fast enough. The alligator's massive jaws sprang open, ready to bite into her.

David caught her beneath the arms and dragged her toward safety as Isaac sprang forward, a knife held high. He jumped onto the back of the alligator. It thrashed, trying to dislodge him, but he held on and stabbed his blade through the creature's skull.

As the alligator stilled, Isaac cast David a look of triumph, and warning.

David tensed, the hairs at the nape of his neck prickling.

"Thank you." Amelia threw her arms around him and hugged him tight. She glanced over her shoulder at Isaac. "Thank you to you both."

Isaac didn't acknowledge her thanks in any way. He simply stared at David, his stance one of challenge.

• • •

"I don't trust him," David admitted as he led Amelia in a circuitous path back to their shelter, both to find more ingredients for the pine pitch and to avoid leaving a blatant trail for Isaac to follow.

"Why?" Amelia asked as she walked beside him. "He seems like a nice enough man. He helped save my life."

"Maybe so." He stopped to scoop up a lump of dried dung lying in the grass, dropping it into the coconut shell that contained the hardened pieces of sap they'd collected by the pond.

"You don't sound convinced."

Probably because he *wasn't* convinced. He'd pulled Amelia out of harm's way before Isaac had jumped onto the alligator's back. Although Isaac had killed the beast, David had gotten the sense that Isaac had an ulterior motive for what he'd done... To flaunt his strength and skill in a show of power that would instill fear or respect. Either would do. "Perhaps I'm being unduly protective, but I would feel better if you stayed by my side until we leave this island."

He looked over at Amelia, her porcelain skin now a golden color that suited her, and her blond hair bleached brighter by the sun. If anything happened to her... David glanced at the tracks they'd left behind. It would be hours before the boat would be fixed and they could row away. He had to take matters in hand.

They reached their camp, and David set the shell down by the charred wood. "Stay here. I'm going to find Isaac."

"What?"

"It would be good to know if his shelter is clear across the island or nearby," he began, then stopped when her confused look remained. He wanted to know if Isaac had weapons. What were his resources? He scratched the side of his jaw, the stubble already starting to grow.

How could he explain his innate distrust of the man to a woman who trusted everyone? "It's just something I need to do."

She hurried to their shelter. "I'll go with you."

"No, I prefer to go al—"

"You said yourself I should stay close to you until we leave this island."

He had, but he could move faster and quieter alone. Although she was right. He wouldn't worry about her as much if she was with him.

Amelia retrieved her stays from the ground inside the hut and began lacing it in place.

"What are you doing?"

"I don't want Isaac seeing me in only a shift again. It's unseemly."

"We're on an island in the middle of the Atlantic. I don't think conventional propriety matters in this case."

"It matters to me," she insisted, her fingers still working the laces.

"You'll be too warm. Besides, I don't plan to drop in for a visit. I simply want to see where he lives."

"To spy on him," she added with a wry twist of her lips as she stepped into an under-petticoat and secured it at her waist.

He let out a long breath. "Yes, I suppose so."

She donned yet another petticoat, her hands making quick work of securing the ties. "I'll feel better if I'm dressed appropriately here on out, in case we see Isaac again."

From the set of her jaw and the conviction in her voice, he knew better than to argue. He waited for her to finish dressing.

Several minutes later, when she'd fully donned her gown and all the accoutrements that went with it, he took her hand and escorted her into the forest. Already a sheen of sweat glistened on her brow. Such a pity. He preferred the simple shift to all the frippery she now wore.

Her gown catching on every twig and leaf, she walked beside him, staring at this and that, her mission different from his. "Where do you think Isaac came from?"

He'd pondered the same thing himself. "He's an escaped slave."

Her eyes rounded. "Did he tell you that?"

"He didn't have to. The whip marks on his front and

back, the scars on his wrists... He was probably brought by ship to work one of the plantations on these islands."

"On *this* island?"

Unlikely. "I haven't explored this entire place, but it isn't large enough to sustain a plantation. The forest covers most of the land. Maybe the next island over... In fact, that would explain why a ship would travel there."

"To transport slaves?"

"That and whatever crop they grow. Tobacco, sugar, or what have you."

When they reached the pond, he stopped to assess the area. He released her hand and searched for any sign of tracks. The alligator was gone. No surprise there. Isaac had hovered by the alligator as he finished filling his gourds with water. David would have taken it for food himself, if he could have, but he suspected that Isaac would have fought tooth and nail if he'd approached the creature. With Amelia so close by, it hadn't been worth the risk, no matter their hunger. They'd find some other way to fill their bellies.

Still, if Isaac had dragged the alligator off, it shouldn't be too difficult to find which direction he'd gone.

"Did your ship ever transport slaves?" she asked, breaking the silence.

"Not that I know of."

Her shoulders relaxed, and a sweet smile curled her lips.

He spied a barely discernible path and waved Amelia to follow. "I wouldn't think *too* highly of *The Wanderer's* crew. They're a lazy sort. It's likely they simply didn't want to burden themselves with the illness and rebellion that comes with a hold full of people."

Her smile didn't dim, and the look she sent his way was

pleased. "Well, I'm glad for it."

Honestly, he was, too. After spending time as a slave himself, he wouldn't have been able to stomach the thought. No man or woman should have to live as someone's property.

Isaac had obviously attempted to cover his tracks, and he'd done a fair job. Even so, David found enough signs to follow. As they started down the trail, he lifted his finger to his lips to signal her silence.

It didn't work.

"I'm curious," she asked. "What language were you speaking…to Isaac?"

"Malagasy. It's the language of Madagascar. Unfortunately, it wasn't much help."

"Can you teach me?"

"I know very little myself, but I can try, if you can stay silent from here on out."

She nodded her assent and followed behind, still taking in her surroundings as if on a leisurely stroll.

Although the forest grew thicker, he spotted a movement ahead. He motioned for Amelia to be still. She, of course, came to stand by his side.

"What do you see?" she whispered.

This time, he covered her lips with his hand and shook his head. Isaac had hidden his tracks, which meant he didn't want to be found. Best to take a peek and be off, before the man realized he had an audience.

David inched forward until Isaac came into view. He squatted by the alligator, his knife cutting into its flesh, slicing off the meat. A sturdy hut half obscured by a tight cluster of trees stood several feet to his right with a fire burning out front. Over the top of the fire, a structure of sticks lashed together held strips of meat hanging out to dry.

Something stirred in the hut, and a woman waddled through the door, her belly distended in pregnancy. Of course. Now he understood Isaac's show of aggression. He wanted to warn away any possible threat. Amelia grabbed his arm as she, too, noticed the woman now walking toward the fire.

Isaac had said he was alone on the island, not that David could blame the man for lying. A pregnant woman to protect out here in the middle of nowhere—he didn't envy him one whit. He glanced over at Amelia. The thought of Amelia with child, no midwife or doctor to help her through labor, brought a sick feeling to his gut.

Time to go. He'd seen enough. If they left Isaac and this woman in peace, most likely he'd be no threat to them. David waved Amelia away, and they slowly backed through the brush. Although David detected no sound from their movements, Isaac's head snapped up. His knife in hand, he rushed toward them.

David stepped forward, placing himself in front of Amelia as Isaac broke through the stand of trees and came to a halt. Surprise flickered over his features before a glare settled in. He hissed out words David didn't understand, but his deepening frown David couldn't mistake. Isaac was none too pleased to see them.

• • •

The furious look on Isaac's face put a soursop-sized lump in Amelia's throat. His scowl didn't soften even when David raised his hands in a display of good will. Isaac yelled in a foreign tongue and swiped his blade before them in warning.

David retreated, nudging her with him, when something rustled the brush behind Isaac, and the woman Amelia had seen come out of the hut moments earlier now peeked from the trees.

"Hello," Amelia called, half stepping out from behind David, only to have him snatch her arm and haul her back.

Isaac shouted at the woman, a terse command she ignored. "I'm called Ruth. What's your name?"

Ruth's accent was unlike anything Amelia had ever heard before. Although she spoke perfect English, her voice had a singsong quality to it that was quite pleasant.

"Amelia," she answered. "This is David."

"Good to meet you." She gestured for them to follow her. "Come. Come."

The warning in Isaac's eyes made them hesitate, until he relented and walked beside Ruth to their camp. He didn't return to the alligator, but stayed close to Ruth's side as she sat down by the fire and gestured for Amelia to do the same. David hovered nearby.

"Isaac told me he saw you at the pond."

Amelia stole a glance at Isaac as he stood behind Ruth, listening intently, although how much he could understand was questionable. "Isaac was very brave. The way he killed that alligator..." She suppressed a shudder at the memory. "Please let him know how thankful we are."

Ruth looked at Isaac and spoke to him in what Amelia could only assume was his native language. Afterward, Isaac nodded toward Amelia, not exactly friendly, but civil, nevertheless.

It was a start, although the curt gesture did little to defuse the tension in the air. She smiled, hoping that would help.

"This is a very nice camp." The well-built hut must have taken some time to erect. As did the dried gourds, clay pots, and woven baskets. "How long have you been on this island?"

"Most a year," Ruth replied, her hands smoothing over her belly.

"That long," Amelia breathed. She couldn't imagine such a thing.

Ruth's gaze dipped to the fashionable gown Amelia wore, a stark contrast to Ruth's simple shirt and skirt, her hair covered by a white handkerchief. Heat rose up Amelia's neck. Apparently she'd overdressed. Yet, she had nothing else to wear that wouldn't be indecent. Still, what did it matter? Ruth would be lovely in anything she wore. "Your eyes." Although Ruth's skin was almost as dark as Isaac's, her eyes were the bluest Amelia had ever seen. "They're extraordinary."

"How are you here?" Ruth asked, ignoring the compliment, a suspicious glint in her eyes.

"I…" Heat rose to her cheeks. How could she explain how a ship of pirates had cast her out to sea?

"We escaped from a pirate ship," David spoke up, saving her from the humiliation of telling the tale herself. Bless him.

"Pirate ship? Here?" A look of skepticism wrinkled Ruth's features, and she spoke to Isaac over her shoulder.

"No." Amelia assured her. "We used a rowboat to get here. The pirate ship never visited."

The disbelief never left Ruth's face. "You rowed to the island from the ocean?"

"Yes, we were *lucky* enough to come upon this island," David explained, giving Amelia a wink.

Yes, indeed they had been. "How about you?" she asked Ruth. "Where are you from?"

Ruth didn't answer. Instead, she spoke to Isaac, who stiffened. One look at the whip marks on his chest and Amelia regretted the question. David's nudge and shake of the head didn't help ease her sudden disquiet. "David was also a slave for a time," she blurted out. If they knew of his experiences…

The cynicism in their stares nearly made her flinch. "It's true. He has a scar on his lower back." She turned to him.

Despite his obvious discomfort, he nodded. "I was a slave in Madagascar."

Ruth and Isaac's expressions didn't change. She fanned her face. It seemed this part of the island was even warmer than theirs. The subject must be a difficult one to discuss. She'd try another. "You've been here a year, don't you miss your family?" Then again, if their families were slaves of some sort… Oh, no. "You must be lonely," she babbled. She pasted a smile into place. "How long before the baby arrives?" How frightening it must be to have no one to help with labor when the time came. Drat! Why couldn't she find some topic more comforting? "You'll soon have the island to yourselves again." Perhaps that would give them relief. "As soon as our boat is fixed, we'll be rowing to an island not far from here."

Her spine growing rigid, Ruth studied Amelia as if seeing her in a new light. "Did you come from there?"

"No, I already told you…"

"We should go." David took Amelia's arm and pulled her up.

"I do hope we can become friends," she called out as David led her into the forest.

Ruth's smile was stiff and wary.

"*Velome*," David said to Isaac as the man followed them to the camp's edge.

"What did you say to him?" Amelia asked as David pulled her along.

"I said, 'Pardon my companion. She doesn't know when to stop talking.'"

"With one word?"

He released a long breath. "I said, 'Good-bye.'"

She stumbled over a clump of dirt in her path. "Did we have to leave in such a rush?" Possibly, if given more time, she would have found some common subject to use as conversation.

"Isaac didn't want us there."

"But Ruth was very nice," she countered.

"Yes—"

"And Isaac helped save my life."

"True enough."

"Then the least we can do is try to extend an olive branch," she insisted, rather wisely, if she did say so herself. She pulled on his hand, ready to return to Ruth and Isaac's camp. "In fact, if we're going to the other island, we could offer to bring back supplies for them."

David tightened his grip. "I don't think that's a good idea."

"Why not?"

"No more talk of going to the other island. If they are escaped slaves from there, they might fear that we'll mention them to the plantation owners."

An outraged gasp escaped. "We'd never do such a thing."

"They don't know that," he argued. "They don't trust us." He released her and picked up a tree branch with a large spray of leaves, then swept it back and forth over any trail they might leave behind.

"Apparently we don't trust them either."

He shrugged. "You're right. I don't."

"We could assure them…" She let that thought fade away. Even she didn't believe they would be convinced by mere assurances.

"Building trust takes time." David arched an eyebrow. "Well, maybe not for you."

She let out a snort. "How amusing you are." And inordinately cautious. The couple they'd just left weren't criminals to be feared. Amelia had faced pirates, for goodness' sake. These two poor people were merely trying to survive, like she and David.

Ruth and Isaac would cause them no trouble. She was sure of it.

Chapter Thirteen

Using a stick, David stirred the melting pine pitch. Its pungent odor was a welcome scent. Once he patched the leak in their boat, they could be on their way with no more worries of what could befall them on this island.

The hard lumps of dried sap dissolved slowly into a thick glue that clung to the sides of the broken conch shell he held over the fire, his hand protected by a palm frond.

Amelia stood in the shallows with a net in her hand. "Where are the God-loving fish?" She bent low and stared into the water. They'd tried catching fish before with no success, but Amelia was determined to try again. He couldn't blame her. Their food choices had been rather limited.

Her flushed face was a fine sight to see, considering how sick she'd been. Now knowing they weren't alone on the island, she was dressed in an odd assemblage of shift, gown, and stays, her under-petticoats too cumbersome to wear in the water. A part of him…his brain…appreciated her actions. The view of her pale shift clinging to her curves would inspire thoughts in his head best kept at bay. Another part of him, a part much lower, wished he could have enjoyed that sumptuous view.

David wiped the perspiration from his forehead with his arm. "You might be scaring the fish away. Stand still." He took in her soaked dress and the water dripping from the lace on her elbow-length sleeves. "I've never seen anyone fish like that. Would you like me to bring you a parasol, my lady?"

Other than a slight scrunch of her nose, she ignored the remark. "I've searched the shore for what has to be going on two hours. There are no fish." She scanned the water, her shoulders slumping. "I'm famished."

She wasn't the only one.

The pitch fully melted, he added crushed charred wood and animal droppings, mixing the lot together. They'd explored the forest for hours looking for a beehive. Beeswax would have added greater pliancy to the pitch, but they'd found none. All that effort wasted. Now nearly dusk, they would soon have no light to forage for food. Although they had happened upon one more soursop, his stomach was beyond growling. Perhaps he *should* have fought Isaac for the alligator.

He glanced at the nymph in the water, her hair curling along her cheeks. Her movements slow as she dragged her dress along, she waded out a little deeper until the water rose to her hips. Her face lit up, and she bent closer to the water's surface once more. "I see one…no, two fish!" Reaching out, she thrust her net forward. "No! Come back." She darted to the side, stumbled two paces, and fell into the water.

David leaped to his feet and had already taken a step when she resurfaced. Sputtering, she lifted the net into the air.

He chuckled at the sight. A five inch beast flopped inside the knotted vines. "Well done."

Out of breath, Amelia struggled to stand, and still she looked like the happiest woman in the world. She radiated joy even as her hair and clothes adhered to her skin. "I can't believe I caught one." Her dazzling smile sparked a warmth inside him that had nothing to do with the fire.

He crouched low to tend to his pitch. "Impressive." And beautiful. Her wet hair glistened in the waning sunlight and dripped along plump lips waiting to be kissed, before draping over bountiful breasts he yearned to... Scalding heat singed his fingertips, and he yanked his hand away. *Damn.* The leaf had caught fire. He flipped the frond into the sand and chose another to protect his fingers from the heat of the shell.

Amelia trudged to the shore and crossed to the fire, where she tossed her catch to the beach, then frowned. "This won't be enough for two." She dripped from head to toe, but paid no heed. He loved that about her, the way she accepted life as it came. No regrets. No objections.

"You should have it." David forced his attention to the pitch, scraping the sides of the shell. "After all, you were the one who caught it."

"I'll catch another." Her gaze took in the pistol at his side before she returned to the water and waded in. She brushed her hair out of her eyes and glanced his way. "Do you really think the pistol is necessary?"

Although he'd seen no sign of Isaac since that morning, better to err on the safe side. "It's merely a precaution." He knew from experience what slavery could do to a man, the distrust it could foster, even against those who didn't deserve it. He hadn't been the only white man enslaved in Madagascar. Months after his capture, he'd seen two others. He'd heard tell that their shipmates had tried to rescue them and failed. Neither had survived long after. Both had died by their master's hand.

David crumbled more charred wood into the pitch and stirred it into the thick, black mixture. After he'd been told of their deaths, a hate had begun to grow, an irrational anger toward all black men, no matter if they'd done wrong to him or not. Fortunately, that madness had dissipated as quickly as it had begun, but he'd seen a flicker of that same hatred and distrust in Isaac's eyes when they'd invaded his home.

A female screech stilled his hands. His gaze darted toward the sea where Amelia held her foot in her hands and wavered on one leg. He sprang to his feet at the sight of the pain on her face. She wobbled until she had to set her foot down, then she stumbled and fell beneath the ocean waves.

"Amelia!" He raced to the water and dove in, rushing to her side.

She was struggling to rise when he scooped her up and carried her to shore. He cradled her against him, his pulse still drumming hard. "What happened?"

Amelia sputtered and coughed as he set her down. Finally regaining her breath, she wheezed, "I tried not to step on it, but the force of a wave pushed me." She took up her foot, and he spied several black projections protruding from the side. Spines. Likely from a sea urchin. One of his shipmates had come into similar trouble. He remembered the pain the wretch had been in and all of his howling and swearing.

Her eyes bright with tears, Amelia grimaced.

"I know it hurts, but I'll need you to hold still." David

bent over the wounds and carefully extracted each spine, the process slow so he wouldn't break it off beneath the skin.

With each tug, new tears fell, but she didn't move, didn't make a sound, save for a few pants for air. His brave girl. When the last was gone, he pulled her close and kissed the top of her wet hair. He murmured soothing words, offering what comfort he could. She felt so good in his arms, he only reluctantly let her go.

Already her wounds had become red and swollen. He placed a coconut shell containing water to the edge of the fire and tore a strip from his shirt. "We'll clean out what poisons remain as soon as the water is hot."

A weak smile brightened her tear-stained cheeks. "The way you abuse that shirt, you'll soon have none of it left."

"I don't give a damn about the shirt. I value you more."

A delicate blush rose to her cheeks, and he savored the sight with his heart and soul. She looked at him with such tenderness, a look that bordered on love. His chest constricted until he could barely breathe. "Let's move you over to the fire," he rasped. He carried her closer and set her down.

The water now hot, he dipped the cloth and held it to her wounds. She hissed in pain at first contact, but soon the tension left her face, and her body relaxed.

He dampened the cloth again and reapplied it to her foot. The worst now passed, his attention wandered up her bare, slender leg. He remembered well the smooth feel of her skin, the sensual way she reacted to his touch, and he longed to glide his hand along that limb again.

When he lifted his gaze, their eyes locked, and the desire reflecting back at him stole every rational thought from his head. He leaned in and savored her lips, the taste salty and sweet, before his senses returned and he drew away. "I'd best return to my pine pitch."

His smile forced, he moved to crouch by the fire and picked up his stirring stick, ignoring the disappointment that flashed over her features—the same disappointment that now weighed down his limbs until he sank to the sand.

Amelia would soon be in England. She would reunite with her family and forget about him. David stirred the pine pitch with vigor, his hand growing tired. If all went well, she'd meet a man worthy of her affection and finally find happiness. Who was he to get in the way of that future? He was a bitter man and a failure in so many ways.

No, he'd do what was best for her. He'd take her to safety and send her back home to a bright future...with a more honorable man than him. The stick broke in his hand, and he muttered an oath.

All he wanted was for Amelia to be safe and happy, dammit. That and to beat every honorable man in England into the dust.

• • •

Amelia rubbed her eyes as she staggered from the foliage where she'd relieved herself. The air humid, she trudged through the brush under the light of the full moon, thankful David had convinced her to sleep in her shift. When her feet met cool powdery sand, a figure in the shadows caught her eye. She squinted to see... Isaac, a knife in his hand, hovered just outside their shelter. Dear God.

She looked around for a weapon. Her pulse taking flight,

she picked up a heavy stick and rushed forward. "David! Wake up!"

Isaac's attention jerked toward her, but he made no move her way. Instead, he ducked under the shelter. No! David! She ran full out, her sore foot a hindrance, and tripped when her legs couldn't keep up with her. She landed in a heap in the sand. Regaining her footing, she grabbed the stick and raced ahead.

Inside the wall-less shelter, David raised the pistol, but Isaac smacked it out of his hands. In a quick move, David unsheathed his dagger and stepped away.

The two men faced each other, their knives out. They took a few swipes, testing the other's reflexes. She didn't wait. As soon as she reached them, she swung her stick.

She struck Isaac in the arm and the back before he turned to her with a wild slash that could have sliced her through if she hadn't jumped to the side. David let out a war cry and barreled forward out of their sleeping place, knocking Isaac into a tree trunk. Isaac's knife fell from his hand, and the two men grappled over David's blade.

Amelia snatched up the knife Isaac had dropped, then remembered… She scanned the sand and found the pistol. David cried out. No! Blood spilled from a wound in his side as Isaac reared back for another strike.

"Stop," she screamed, the pistol pointed at his nose, close enough to ensure she wouldn't miss, but at a distance he couldn't reach. "Get away from him!"

Isaac slid on his backside, putting several feet between them, his eyes wide.

Her arm shook. She wished she could shoot, but killing a man… She couldn't. "Go!"

He flinched, then rose to his feet and ran into the forest, leaving David leaning against the tree trunk, clutching his side with bloodied fingers.

"David." She fell to her knees beside him, the pistol gripped in one hand as she jumped at every sound around them. Would Isaac return?

Her vision blurred as tears spilled from her eyes. David had taken precautions. All day he'd been watchful, his knife or pistol always at hand. She'd thought him foolish. Now...

"Amelia." David grabbed her hand and squeezed. "It's going to be fine," he groaned.

Amelia raced into the shelter and brought back her petticoat, in time to see a coconut drop from the tree above David. It hit him on the head, and he slumped to his side. Her jaw fell open. "That hadn't just... Not possible." The familiar cold fingers of dread clamped down on her shoulders. Bad luck. Extremely bad luck.

She shook the thought away. No time for that now. "We need to move you out from under there." She rushed to his side, peering up to make sure nothing more would fall. David blinked slowly, but helped her as she moved him several feet from the tree. After a quick inspection of his head, which revealed a growing lump but no blood, she tore off a large piece of the petticoat, followed by a long strip. So much blood. She pressed the cloth to his side and bound the injury with the strip, then scanned the trees for any sign of Isaac. They had to leave here, and soon. He'd surely try to attack again.

Amelia rushed to gather their things, although they hadn't a lot to take. The pistol, David's knife, her gown, and his violin. She placed them in the rowboat and tried to push it across the sand to no avail. Her feet digging in the sand, she dragged the thing inch by inch until she reached the shore, her lungs heaving and her injured foot throbbing.

She found David with his eyes closed, his hand resting loosely on his wound. "David?" Her blood ran cold when he didn't stir. She grabbed him by both shoulders and shook him. "David!"

His lids fluttered open, revealing those beautiful brown eyes. A feeble smile came to his lips. "It's going to be fine."

Would it? She checked his wound. The bleeding had slowed to a trickle. Thank heavens. She held his face in her hands, bringing his attention to her. "We're leaving. I have to get you up, and I'll need your help."

At his nod, she wrapped his arm around her neck and pulled him to a sitting position. "Ready?" she asked, but didn't wait for an answer before using all her strength and some of his to get him to his feet. He hissed with the movement, but soon stood.

They shuffled forward, each step making him wince anew. When they finally reached the boat, she helped him inside and pressed a new piece of cloth from her petticoat to the wound. The bleeding had grown worse, but she could waste no more time.

Straining until her muscles ached, she pulled and pushed until the rowboat was free from shore, then climbed in and took up the oars. David's head lolled against the side of the boat. "David," she called, steering them into the waves, her movements awkward.

His eyes opened a crack, and he blinked.

"Stay awake." She almost whimpered the request as the hopelessness of their situation threatened to weaken her will. "Please. I need you."

Those few words seemed to have an effect. David's eyes opened a bit more, and he tried to smile. She rowed through another wave, fighting the water's insistence to send them back to shore, or flip them over. Lord help them if they flipped. She couldn't even swim. And David... Stop. She had to focus on David, not on what could happen. Given his head injury, she'd best keep him alert, but how? Her mind turned to the obvious—the question that plagued her. "Why would Isaac attack us? We were nothing but friendly."

"I don't blame him," David muttered as he tried to sit up higher. He succeeded, but groaned in the process.

A strange thought coming from him. He saw the world in a dim light, ready to believe the evils of men. "Why not?"

"When I finally escaped my master, I would have done anything to prevent my recapture." He huffed out a short exhale. "I *did* do things I now regret."

Yes, the man he killed whom he thought to be a guard. "But we're no threat to him or Ruth."

"He may see it differently."

"I don't understand." Her arms grew tired the more she rowed, although her strokes had improved. At least the waves had stopped trying to turn the boat since they'd reached calmer waters.

David blinked slowly. "The way he looked at your dress, with distrust. I'm sure the plantation wives wear much the same."

Her dress? She'd felt the tension when they'd spoken with Isaac and Ruth, but... "It was me he had an issue with?"

When he shook his head, it barely moved. "They didn't accept our story of a pirate ship, and the more likely place we would have come from is the other island... We asked so many questions about them… If we told anyone about Isaac and Ruth, they could be caught." His eyes closed again.

"David?"

He didn't respond, and her heart squeezed so hard, she could barely draw air.

"David." She bent over him, her cheek to his mouth. He still breathed. Her fingers shaking, she lifted the cloth now spotted with blood. His wound had stopped bleeding. Good.

Resuming her position, Amelia grabbed hold of the oars and rowed as fast as possible. *She'd* been the one who'd asked Isaac and Ruth questions they hadn't wanted to answer. *She'd* been the one who'd insisted she wear the blasted dress. *She'd* told David they were no threat, convincing him to wait until morning before using their newly repaired boat—he'd looked so tired. She should be the one lying unconscious on the far side of the boat, not David. Never David.

Clenching her jaw tight, she resisted the urge to cry, although the tears clogged her throat. She had to stay strong and focus on getting David to a doctor. If the neighboring island had a plantation, they probably had access to a physician.

The thought of losing David, of his…death. She couldn't bear it. She wouldn't let that happen. She rowed harder, ignoring the way her muscles burned. David would survive this, and she would travel to her aunt just as she'd planned from the first.

She watched David's chest rise and fall with each breath. He'd be better off without her. She stared at his handsome face, the lips she'd kissed so ardently. She memorized his every feature, dark brows that quirked in curiosity, a stubbled jaw that grew rigid with frustration.

A tear escaped the corner of her eye. She'd miss him terribly. Already the familiar loneliness was settling in. No, not only loneliness this time, an ache of such enormity, she could hardly feel anything else. She loved him. She'd told herself time and again she couldn't love him and wouldn't, but in truth she'd had no choice in the matter. Her heart had whispered his name since the moment he'd vowed to protect her. What use in denying it any longer?

Still, it changed nothing. Once David was well, she'd be on her way.

Her shift was drenched in sweat and David's blood, and the pain in her arms became almost unbearable by the time she reached sight of a ship moored offshore. So close. She forced her arms to move, although each stroke brought a low groan to her throat. The pier came into view, a shadow in the moonlight. Off to its side stood a man holding a lantern. Her destination in sight, she rowed all the faster until she drew up alongside the pier.

Dressed in a worn suit, his belly straining the buttons of his vest, the man with the lantern met her there. "Where have you come from?" he asked.

"No time to explain. I need a doctor." She gestured toward David. "He's been stabbed."

His curious eyes took in her meager shift, but he nodded. "I'll get a wagon," he said, then rushed away.

While she waited for his return, she checked David's wound and smoothed his hair from his forehead. "We'll get you to a doctor soon, and then you'll be on the mend. I'm sure of it."

The lie didn't set well on her tongue. She wasn't sure of anything, but she had hope. At least they were here.

Wagon wheels rattled and thumped along the pier. The man climbed from the driver's seat and helped her lift David from the boat and into the wagon bed. She sat next to David, holding the cloth to his wound as they were jostled with every bump and divot in the road.

They passed by fields of tall grasses before they reached a small town. Several buildings lined either side of the street. The wagon stopped before one that was two stories tall and covered in stucco. The man leaped from the driver's seat and rushed to the entrance. "Doc Hale," he shouted, pounding on the door. "Doc Hale!"

A servant with rich brown skin and a slightly rumpled suit answered.

"We need Doc Hale," the driver told him before the servant had a chance to issue a greeting.

The servant disappeared for a matter of minutes before a disheveled, balding man came to the door, buttoning his waistcoat. "What is it, Henry?" he asked.

Henry motioned him toward the back of the wagon. "Over here."

Doctor Hale took one look at David and the bloody piece of petticoat covering his wound and climbed into the wagon. "Well come on then, Henry. Help me get him inside."

The doctor hoisted David's upper body while Henry took his legs, and together they carried him into the building. Judging by the furnishings, she could only assume this was the doctor's home. Amelia followed on their heels, ignoring all else but the man in their arms. David roused enough to groan once before slipping back into unconsciousness. Soon they set him on a bed in a main floor room and the doctor hovered over him, taking a good look at the wound. "How long ago did this injury happen?"

"I'm not sure." Rowing here had taken longer than she'd hoped. "An hour?"

"Came in on a rowboat, she did," Henry explained.

The doctor gave a grunt and glanced her way. In just her shift, blood covering a good deal of the front, she crossed her arms over her chest. If he found her attire strange, he didn't say so. Instead, he rifled through a dresser drawer, bringing forth a thread and needle. "You can go now, Henry."

Henry bobbed his head and turned to leave. "I should be getting back to the night watch."

"Thank you for your help," she said to him before he reached the door.

His gaze darted toward her and then away as quickly as it had come. "No thanks needed."

The doctor set to work stitching David's wound closed. "Rowed a boat here," he muttered. "Where did you come from?"

Worry set her pulse to a rapid pace. "The island just east of here." Not that it mattered. "Will he recover?"

"Hard to know for sure," the doctor said as he tied off the string. "No trouble breathing, no blood in the mouth… If he was bleeding internally, he would have bled to death by now. I'd say his chances are good."

Frustration welled up, but she choked it back down. Medicine wasn't an exact science. She only wished he could tell her for certain. Footsteps approached from behind her, and Amelia looked at a woman about her own size with blond hair swept up beneath an intricate lace cap. The streaks of gray in her hair and the slight lines on her face placed her near Amelia's stepmother's age.

"Hello, I'm Mrs. Margaret Hale." As soon as Mrs. Hale's blue eyes caught sight of Amelia, she laid a hand to her chest. "Oh my. We'd best find you something to wear." She took Amelia by the shoulders and ushered her toward the door. "This way, my dear."

Amelia resisted. "But David."

Mrs. Hale would not be dissuaded. "We'll return as soon as you're properly dressed and cleaned up."

Amelia stared down at her stained shift and the blood that coated her arms and hands.

"Come now," Mrs. Hale insisted, tugging her arm firmly. "We'll only be a few minutes."

"Don't worry," the doctor added. "He's extremely fortunate. If the knife had cut a major organ or artery, he would have died by now."

Fortunate? He'd been stabbed. With a sigh, she let the woman lead her away. David's luck had gone dry the moment he'd met her. He likely wouldn't have been stabbed at all if she hadn't been there. She quelled a dry laugh. Of course he wouldn't have been stabbed. If they'd never met, he wouldn't have abandoned his ship and been stranded on an island with a man so distrustful, he'd rather lash out than extend a hand in friendship.

She followed Mrs. Hale up to the second floor and into a bedroom, the guilt building with every step, her stepmother's words ringing true once more. Poor judgment, bad luck. They followed her like a plague, infecting everyone she came into contact with.

"There's water on the table in the corner. You can use it to wash up." Mrs. Hale moved to the wardrobe and searched within.

"Thank you." Amelia poured water from the ewer into the basin and tried to wash off the blood, using a scrap of soap from the table. David's blood. Her hands shook as she scrubbed harder, the soap scraping against her skin. *David will not die. I will not be the cause of his death.* She should leave. David would be safe here with the doctor. She shuffled from foot to foot, the urge to flee strong.

"Here we are." Mrs. Hale laid out a fresh shift on the bed, along with a sturdy pale green gown. "This should fit you well enough, but you'll need an under-petticoat and stays. *Hmm.*"

"I have my own. They're in the boat down at the pier." She gasped for air as a wave of heat overwhelmed her.

"Yes. I'll have someone fetch your things for you, but in the meantime…" Mrs. Hale rifled through a chest along the far wall. "Poor girl. You look like you've been through quite the ordeal."

If she only knew. "Would you tell me about this island?" Amelia asked as she changed into the fresh shift.

Mrs. Hale arched a brow. "What do you want to know?"

"Are there any uninhabited places? On the opposite side perhaps."

"Yes, no one that I know strays beyond the plantation and town." Mrs. Hale handed over worn stays then returned to the chest and dug inside. "Why would you ask?"

Amelia hurried to tie the stays in place, her fingers tingling. "No reason. From a distance, this place appears desolate."

"*Mmm.*" Mrs. Hale brought over a petticoat, wrinkled from its time in the chest. "Have you and your…brother traveled far?"

She ignored the question in Mrs. Hale's voice regarding whether David was her brother or something else. "The ship we traveled on sank, leaving us stranded on the ocean for days." The half lie would have to do. No point in mentioning that David had been a pirate as it might not settle too well, and he'd need the help of the doctor and his wife until he healed.

Amelia hurried to dress, eager to see David again. She would make sure he was in good hands…before she left. The thought robbed her of breath and produced an ache in her heart she feared would never go away.

As Mrs. Hale escorted her downstairs, the sun peeked through the windows with the start of a new day. The doctor was nowhere in sight, and Mrs. Hale left to find him. The dawn's rays bathed David's face as he lay on the bed. A man so strong and stubborn, now fighting for his very life.

Although she longed to pace, to move, she touched her palm to his face, his whiskers prickly. "I love you," she whispered. She had to tell him just once, even if he couldn't hear it.

"Amelia?" His eyes opened, his lids heavy and his gaze unfocused.

Her heart leaped. "I'm here," she said, then winced. *But not for long.*

The corner of his lips rose in a smile that warmed her through and through. She had so much she wanted to say to him. She wanted to thank him for all he'd done for her, the support he'd given, the encouragement, but the words wouldn't come. Tears stung her eyes, and her voice wavered. "I have to go."

His eyes drifted closed, and her tears fell. David had lasted through the night. He'd recover with the help of the doctor. Then he could find *The Wanderer* once again. He'd be safe if she left his side. He'd be safe. That thought locked in her mind, she headed for the door. Once outside, she raced toward the edge of town, then gave in to the impulse to run. Although her injured foot ached with each step she took, she ran as far and as fast as her legs could go.

Chapter Fourteen

David awoke with a start, blinking rapidly to bring the world into focus. Something wasn't right. An anchor-sized knot twisted in his gut, and a sense of loss pervaded his chest. *Amelia.* He attempted to sit up and pain sliced through his side, forcing him to lie back. He held his hand over the pained spot, a bandage beneath his fingers, and scanned the room. "Amelia?"

A balding man came through the door. "Good. You're awake. I'm Dr. Hale."

"Where am I?"

"Caldwell Island." The doctor checked beneath David's bandage. "And this," he gestured toward the doorway where another man stood, "is Robert Caldwell."

David ignored Caldwell and groaned as the doctor pressed his fingers around the wound. "Where's Amelia?"

"Ah, the girl. Haven't seen her since early this morning." The doctor reapplied the bandage and settled a hand on David's forehead. "Don't worry. We're on an island. She couldn't have gone far."

"I have a few questions." Mr. Caldwell stepped inside the room with the confidence of a man who owned the place and everyone inside. He removed his hat and wiped his brow with a handkerchief. Although the day wasn't yet excessively warm, the portly man already had a sheen of sweat coating his skin. "I've been told you came from the neighboring island."

Had he? He remembered very little of the prior night. Although…yes, Amelia had helped him into a boat.

"Did you see anyone else while you were there?" Mr. Caldwell asked.

Isaac and Ruth. Mr. Caldwell of Caldwell Island must be the plantation owner. David shook his head. "No, no one."

Mr. Caldwell's blue eyes narrowed, his crow's-feet deepening. "Are you saying this girl, Amelia, stabbed you?"

A vehement denial sprang to his lips, but he held it back. Caldwell's insinuation was clear. If she didn't do it, then who did? He wouldn't have stabbed himself. "It was an accident. She didn't mean to hurt me." Placing the blame on her soured his stomach, but what else could he do?

A smirk stretched Caldwell's lips. "An accident? How did it happen?"

"She slipped." He would say no more. Better the lie be a short one. "Now if you'll excuse me…" He attempted to sit up once again.

The doctor pressed him down. "You should rest."

He couldn't rest. Amelia wouldn't simply leave him in order to explore the town. A memory came back, a hazy one. Amelia by his bed with tears in her eyes, telling him…she had to go. His heart crashed to the floor. But where would she go, and why?

"You're lying," Caldwell insisted. "I'm looking for two escaped slaves. Where are they hiding?"

He had no time for this. He had to find Amelia. "Unhand me," he ordered the doctor, who pursed his lips and stepped away. David pushed himself up into a sitting position, his side burning with the effort.

"My men searched that island a year ago. Where did you see my slaves last?" Caldwell demanded as David struggled to rise.

Once on his feet, David drew in a long breath, and promptly passed out cold.

. . .

Amelia trudged through the foliage, the forest more dense than the one they'd passed through on the other island. While her pulse had calmed to a steady rhythm, her nerves still hummed. She'd been walking for hours, or so it seemed, and still the need to escape propelled her forward.

Seeing David covered in blood, unable to open his eyes… She shuddered and nearly tripped as she stepped over a fallen tree. Her throat tightened and her eyelids prickled at the thought of the man she'd left behind. To never see him again… The ground blurred as tears filled her eyes.

Drenched in sweat, Amelia broke through the trees to a deserted sandy beach. Blue water and pale sand, coconut trees—she'd seen it all before, although the colors here were less vibrant and the heat less bearable. Even the sun had dulled without David's presence. How she yearned to run back to him.

If David were here, he'd say she was being foolish, that

her curse was nothing but a misguided theory based on malicious lies. That she placed too much importance on her every misfortune and poor decision. But this time, the things she'd said, the things she'd done to prompt Isaac to attack… David had been stabbed, and a coconut had fallen on his head!

She approached the water's edge and rubbed her face with her hands. Although he was so far away, she could hear David's voice in her head, reminding her that she'd experienced good luck as well as bad. Amelia inhaled a large breath and dropped her hands from her face. He'd been right on that count. She'd been most fortunate to know him.

Her stepmother had instilled the belief in curses and bad luck, and David had suspected jealousy as the cause. Once again, she had to agree. Her relationship with her father had never been the same after her stepmother had spread her poison.

She stared out at the water, the vast blue ocean stretching out as far as she could see, and her gaze caught on a sight to her far left. A ship moored just off the island. No pirate flag. Perhaps a trading ship, but what was it doing here instead of at port? She returned to the line of trees and followed the edge. Peeking between the foliage, she watched a longboat heading to shore.

By the time she crept up to the far side of the beach, the boat had been grounded and a handful of people were disembarking. Among them was a woman, her stomach slightly rounded. A tall man with ink-black hair helped her alight from the boat. The man looked vaguely familiar. They walked toward Amelia as she crouched in the scrub.

"Are you sure you'll be comfortable here?" the man

asked.

The woman smoothed her hand over his coat, her head cocked at an angle. "James, I'll have Dr. Newsome, Whip, and the guards to watch over me. Besides, you'll be returning by nightfall."

James nodded. "I will. I promise." He took her hand and dropped a kiss on her knuckles. "I just hate leaving you here even for a short time. If I could take you with me, I would."

A smile touched the woman's lips. "Believe me, I have no desire to return to New Providence. Now go. I'll be fine."

The man released a long exhale and shook his head as if he would change his mind.

"James Lamont," she scolded. "We've traveled for months searching for your brother. You can't stop now."

James Lamont? Searching for his brother? David. Amelia smothered a gasp. Was that why James had looked familiar? For once, she'd come across good fortune.

For once? Was that true? David would argue that she'd had good fortune all along. Perhaps he was right. After all, she had found help getting David to the doctor when she'd needed it most, and David had survived a serious knife wound, for goodness' sake.

"You're right." James kissed the woman's cheek and headed for the boat.

"Wait!" Amelia rushed from her hiding place before James could get away.

Hands dove for pistols and swords at her sudden appearance, but none were drawn. James hurried back to the woman's side. "Who are you, and what do you want?" he asked Amelia, his eyes searching the area behind her. "Who else is with you?"

Amelia raised her hands as a show of good faith. "I'm

alone." A pang of sadness clutched her heart at the reminder.

James's brows drew low in disbelief.

"Truly, I'm alone," she insisted. "And I know where you can find your brother David."

"New Providence," James supplied. "We've heard that's where *The Wanderer* has gone."

"David is no longer on *The Wanderer*. He's here on this island."

James took a step toward her, an earnest look on his face. "How do you know all this?"

Because she'd been rescued by those same pirates, by David. If she were truly bad luck, she would have drowned on *Fortune's Song*. "He left *The Wanderer* for me. We've been traveling together, and I brought him here because he's been injured."

Shocked expressions greeted her all around, and she rushed to add, "He's recovering. I brought him to a doctor who lives in the town on the other side of this island." Not that David's survival had anything to do with medicine. Dr. Hale had done little more than stitch him up.

She gazed at David's brother, who'd traveled so far with the unlikeliest odds of ever finding David. "What brought you here?" They could have chosen to land on the neighboring island or on the other side of this one. Why here? Why now?

James shrugged and turned to the woman at his right. "Lady's choice. I left the decision up to my wife."

A becoming blush pinkened Mrs. Lamont's cheeks. "I don't have a good reason for choosing this place over another. I suppose you could say something drew me here."

They'd come here by chance. One could say by luck. A weight lifted from Amelia's shoulders.

A curious look swept over Mrs. Lamont's face. "If you've been traveling with David, what are you doing here alone?"

The truth became as clear as the ocean water around them. She did have good fortune. Well, good and bad, like everyone did. Meeting David proved that beyond all else. With him, she'd found love, which made her the luckiest woman of all.

Her lips curved in a bright smile, and the thought of seeing David again made her breathless. "The reason why I'm alone here doesn't matter anymore. Let's go see David."

• • •

Already afternoon, and still Amelia hadn't returned. "I've walked your corridors for the last half hour. I've eaten and had plenty of water. I'm feeling fine," David lied. "Short of tying me down, you won't be keeping me here a moment longer."

Dr. Hale scowled. "Do what you must, but if you lose consciousness or break open your stitches—"

"I won't blame you," David finished for him. Tucking in the tails of the shirt Mrs. Hale had given him, he ignored the discomfort each movement caused. As for the light-headedness, it came and went less frequently than it had during the morning hours. He headed for the door, thankful to finally leave the sickbed and begin his search for Amelia. Where could she be?

He spied a flash of pale green in the hall, and before he could reach the corridor, Amelia was there in the doorway. Thank God.

A happy grin lit her face as she rushed forward. "You're up."

He met her within a few steps, and his injury be damned, he wrapped his arms around her and squeezed. "Where have you been?"

"Don't worry about where I've been." She gestured toward the door. "Look who I've found."

David peered over her head. *James?* His hold on Amelia loosened, and she stepped away to make room for the others to join them. Behind James was a woman, trailed by Thomas and Whip, James's trusty crewmen. Thomas nodded toward David, while the old man Whip displayed a toothy grin. "Where you been, sprat?"

"How did you find me?" David asked, his voice barely more than a breath.

James gave a harsh laugh. "Through a combination of perseverance and luck. I've sailed all over the world searching for you."

He had?

"We traveled to Madagascar, then heard tell you'd joined a ship headed this way, so we followed." James's golden eyes, so much like their father's, glistened. "Good Lord, it's good to see you." He closed the distance between them and clasped David in a hug so strong, David grunted from both emotion and pain.

"Sorry." James backed up a step. "I heard you were injured."

"It's nothing," David assured him. At least nothing that would kill him.

David looked past his brother, and James hurried to introduce the woman at his side. "This is my wife, Mrs. Charity Lamont."

Wife? And a pregnant one at that. "When did this happen?"

Charity's loving gaze turned to her husband, and James's

smile grew. "We'll have plenty of time to talk about it on our way to London."

David froze, and the relief at seeing his brother faded away. "I'm not going back." He'd made up his mind on that months ago.

"What?" James asked. "Why not?"

"I don't belong there anymore." He didn't care if he ever saw his father again. Gordon Lamont had never believed his second son was worth the air he breathed. What would his father think of him now? He'd spent time as a pirate and a slave. He'd murdered an innocent man. A strong mixture of anger and shame burned in his gut. No, he could never face his father again.

James stepped forward. "I haven't been searching for more than a year to return empty-handed."

"And I appreciate that you searched for me, but—"

"Think of our sisters," James argued, his voice growing louder. "They've been beside themselves with worry."

"You can assure them I'm safe and well." He was a selfish bastard. He couldn't deny it, but while he missed his sisters and James, his life wasn't in London anymore.

"David," James growled. His wife Charity rested a comforting hand on James's arm, and he inhaled a deep breath, his jaw rigid.

David shook his head. "Unless you plan to take me as your prisoner, I'm not going."

"How about to Sussex then?" Amelia still stood by David's side, but the joy that had bathed her face when she'd first returned had disappeared. "When I left here today, believing I'd never see you again...it forced me to think things through, such as why I'd left the man I love."

She loved him? His heart drummed hard in his chest.

Amelia glanced warily at the others in the room and lowered her voice. "I took a good look at my beliefs, at the curse—your reasons disclaiming it, those things I blamed myself for, and all the good fortune that has come my way." She took his hand in hers, the sincerity in her eyes robbing him of breath. "You were right all along. The curse doesn't exist. I need to go back to my family. I kept myself at a distance from my father and sister for so long, and through it all they were patient and kind. I need to make amends, and let them know how very much I care."

As she should, but not with him. He gazed into her blue-green eyes, the glint of hope shining there something he'd yearned to see for the longest time. Now that her so-called curse was no longer holding her back, the world was open to her like never before. She could do anything with her life, with an honorable man by her side, a man more honorable than he could ever be. But she'd escaped from pirates. If anyone found out, they'd see her as ruined. And she was no longer an innocent. Curse it. He'd seen to that.

More arguments rushed to the fore, but he pushed them aside. She'd be fine. Who would know what had transpired while she'd traveled at sea? No doubt Captain Tuttlage and his crew were from London, near the port, and soon they would be sailing again, her secret safe. Besides, her family would protect her, and anyone truly worthy of her would value her despite it all. No, she would have a better life without him.

"David, come with me," she pleaded. "Please."

His chest squeezed. "I can't," he rasped. His throat closed off as if trying to keep him from saying what he must. They'd always planned to go their separate ways. The fact that she was going to England instead of Virginia changed nothing. He swallowed to relieve the tightness in his throat. "I wish you well."

Amelia held David's hand in a viselike grip. "I can go, stay for a short while, and then return."

"I won't be here." Although his insides threatened to combust, he held firm. She deserved more. So kind and sweet, she deserved nothing but the best.

Tears sparkled in her eyes. "I—I could stay with you." Even as she said the words, a look of pain crossed her features. She needed to return to her family.

David rubbed his hand over the back of his neck, willing himself to stay strong. "I'm going to find *The Wanderer*. They were headed to New Providence before they took on the captives. After they ransom the lot, I would bet they'll return, and by my estimates, New Providence isn't far from here."

"No. H-how will you even get there?" A tear broke free and rolled down her cheek.

"I'll find a way." He couldn't resist. He reached out and wiped it from her face. "I'm going to be fine, and so will you." The lie burned his tongue. He'd never be fine again, but Amelia... She would be safe with her family, and some day would start one of her own. The thought of Amelia with another man... He clenched his teeth and dropped his hand from her face. "Now go. All of you."

"Dr. Hale." Mrs. Hale rushed through the door to her husband's side. "You're needed at the plantation."

"What's happened?" the doctor asked, already putting supplies into a bag.

"Mr. Caldwell sent men to the island not far from here, and they found Ruth and Isaac," Mrs. Hale explained. "He's administering Isaac's punishment now."

Dread slithered up David's spine like a snake. Isaac and Ruth had been captured. He remembered well what that was like. And the punishments...

Dr. Hale blew out a sigh and closed his satchel. "Have the carriage brought around."

"It's already done," Mrs. Hale said as she left the room.

"I'm coming with you," David declared. While he had no idea what he'd do once he got there, he couldn't stand by and do nothing.

"Take Mrs. Lamont and Miss Archer back to our ship," James told his men. "I'm going with my brother."

Charity settled a hand on her stomach and nodded.

David opened his mouth to argue, and James pinned him with a stern look. "I'm not done talking to you," James insisted.

"I'll be going, too." This time Amelia spoke.

"No," both men said as one.

She straightened her spine. "Neither of you have a say in this." Her stare hardened as she glanced at David. "I have as much interest in what happens to Ruth and Isaac as you do. Now lead the way."

Chapter Fifteen

Despite David's arguments, Amelia and James sat in the carriage with him and the doctor. The two of them should have returned to James's ship.

The ride was a short one. Soon they passed by fields of sugar cane. An enormous manor made of stone came into view, and in front stood a mass of people witnessing Isaac's punishment. The hair at the nape of David's neck stood on end.

Slaves and overseer alike watched as Mr. Caldwell slashed at Isaac's bare back with a cat-o'-nine-tails. Bound to a tree trunk, Isaac shuddered with each blow, but held his silence.

They reached the edge of the crowd, and the carriage pulled to a stop. "Now don't cause any trouble," the doctor warned before he stepped from the vehicle. "This is plantation business."

Plantation business? This was torture. "Stay with the carriage, Amelia," David said over his shoulder as he leaped to the ground and followed Dr. Hale, with James at his side.

Caldwell had taken off his surcoat. His shirt and vest were drenched in sweat as he pulled his arm back for another strike. All the while, Isaac waited stoically, his feet planted firmly on the ground and blood dripping from the fresh stripes on his skin.

Fury scorched through David like a fire, eager to destroy anything in its path. What made Caldwell so superior that he could own men? That he could punish them for wanting to be free to live their lives in their own way?

"Please, stop," Ruth begged, grabbing hold of Caldwell's arm, tears streaming down her cheeks. "Please!"

David quickened his pace. The need to do something rode him hard, as a memory flashed into his mind's eye. His hands and feet tied to stakes in the ground, while a branch scored the soles of his feet. Sharp stinging pain that had burned for days after.

"Off!" Caldwell threw Ruth off his arm, knocking her to the ground. She cried out and clutched her belly as Isaac bellowed and pulled against his restraints. Isaac's frustration and anger sank into David's skin as if it were his own. His protective instincts rose, and he turned in Ruth's direction, despite the overwhelming compulsion to stop the whipping, no matter what he had to do.

Amelia reached Ruth first. *Bloody hell.* "I told you to stay with the carriage."

She ignored him and attended to Ruth. Dr. Hale approached them, although his attention remained focused on Caldwell. "If you're not careful, you'll hurt your—"

"Don't you dare," Caldwell snapped.

Grandchild? The thought barely penetrated. Yet it made perfect sense…Ruth's blue eyes.

"That woman and her child are slaves, nothing more," Caldwell sneered, his whip meeting its mark again.

David's focus returned to Isaac and the brutality he couldn't abide. Never again. No man should have to live in fear of breaking someone else's rules, to suffer pain for taking control of his life.

Behind him, the doctor persisted. "Then why have you hunted for her so relentlessly?" he asked Caldwell.

Caldwell's voice grew sharp. "You'd be wise to hold your tongue, Dr. Hale."

Mere feet from where Isaac stood, David met Isaac's eyes. Their gazes locked with understanding.

"You there," Caldwell shouted. "Stand back."

An overseer seized David's shoulder, and David pushed him away. When the man grabbed for him again, he slammed his fist into the overseer's jaw, knocking him to his arse. More of Caldwell's men moved forward.

No matter. No one would stop him. David yanked his knife from its sheath and slashed the ropes that bound Isaac's hands, then turned to face those who dared try and stop him.

Isaac let out a guttural roar and charged toward Caldwell. A whip snapped and a group of Caldwell's men rushed Isaac. He fought with the strength of ten men, a wild look in his eye and fury straining his features.

David had no time to watch the spectacle. Two of the overseers stepped forward to detain him. One held a switch and the other a cudgel. Although his side burned from the fighting he'd already done, he prepared for more to come, but before the men could use their weapons, James stepped to David's side.

"What are you doing?" David shouted. "This isn't your

fight."

James pulled a pistol from his belt. "From what I can see, this isn't your fight, either."

In that, James was wrong. After months of captivity and years of his father's bullying, freeing Isaac was something he had to do, to cleanse his soul. He had to fight for justice and freedom, even if it wasn't his own.

The gun held off the overseers, at least for the moment, and James and David backed away when a howl of pain rose up. Three overseers ripped Isaac from Caldwell, who now lay sprawled on the ground, his lifeless eyes staring off in the distance. A bloody rock dropped from Isaac's hand.

The slaves around them glanced from one to the other in shock and amazement, with hope. Almost as one, shouts rose up and the crowd surged forward, attacking the overseers with a ferocity like nothing David had ever seen before.

Within minutes, their rage and resentment turned on everyone in their paths. *Amelia.* His heart knocking against his ribs, David rushed to her side. "We have to go."

From the corner of his eye, David spotted Isaac racing toward them, his attention centered on Ruth who still lay on the ground. Isaac glanced up. All anger was gone, replaced by panic.

David helped him get Ruth to her feet. "Come." He waved them to follow. "You'll be safe with us." They trailed behind him as he led them to the carriage, defending against the few attacks that came their way.

James joined them with the bruised doctor in tow.

"Did Caldwell have family, a wife and children?" David asked, looking up at the massive home that was now under siege.

"He does, but they're off visiting relatives in England," Dr. Hale assured him.

"Good." He didn't relish the thought of what a rescue attempt would entail, and he had no desire to battle slaves in order to save those who lived upon the profits of slave labor. David helped Amelia into the carriage, and then Ruth. The men climbed in after, the fit tight, and the vehicle lurched forward.

"Would you be willing to take Ruth and Isaac aboard?" David asked James. Harboring fugitive slaves was a punishable offense.

Without hesitation, James nodded.

"Ruth..." David appealed to the one who knew English best. "You and Isaac need to leave this place. My brother can take you anywhere you want to go."

"There's a doctor on board my ship who can tend to Isaac's wounds," James added.

Tears glistened in Ruth's eyes. "Thank you." Her stare flitted between James and David. "Thank you both." She spoke to Isaac in a foreign tongue, and a surprised look overcame Isaac's features, followed by relief.

The carriage came to a stop at the pier. Isaac and Ruth alighted, assisted by James.

"I have to be off," Dr. Hale insisted, alarm straining his features. "Mrs. Hale is alone, and this revolt will soon spread to town."

"Thank you for treating David," Amelia said with a slight smile. "And thank your wife for the clothes."

David stepped down to the ground and raised his hand for Amelia.

She settled her hand in his, her smile fading. "Come with

us, David."

His stomach turned to stone. "I can't," he said, forcing the reply past his lips and escorting her to shore, determined to see this through.

"Why not?" The pain in her eyes tore at him. "I love you. We belong together."

Her words pierced his heart. He yearned to draw her close and kiss her sweet lips and soothe the pain he'd caused, but if he did, he wouldn't be able to let her go. Instead, he opened his mouth to explain.

"Don't trouble yourself. I know why," she choked out before he could speak, a glint of anger flashing in her eyes.

"You deserve—"

"No." Her hand squeezed his hard. "Don't say it."

The smell of smoke hung in the air, and the sky over the plantation turned gray.

He had to get Amelia out of here and fast. "I want what's best for you, and that's not me." David gestured toward the longboat and rested a hand on her back, but she dug her heels into the sand and stood her ground.

"You're a good man whether you choose to believe it or not." She peered at the water as if searching for the right thing to say.

"Hurry," James commanded. "We have to shove off."

They didn't have time for this, and whatever she had to say wouldn't make a difference. He scooped her up and carried her to the longboat, the pain in his side a twinge compared to the one in his chest. "We always knew we would go down separate paths eventually. The time has come."

He waded into the water and set her down on a seat, although deep in his heart, he didn't want to release her. Not yet. Not ever. Her eyes frantic, she glanced at the occupants of the boat, her gaze landing on the slaves inside. "David, I don't care what mistakes you've made in the past. Look at Isaac. You don't seem to have any qualms about Isaac loving Ruth. And yet, can't you see how alike the two of you are? Each of you, once slaves, erroneously attacking the innocent in order to ensure your continued freedom." She drew in a wavering breath, her eyes bright with tears. "He's going to spend his life with Ruth. Why can't you spend yours with me?"

"Good-bye, Amelia." David grabbed the edge of the boat, ready to push it from the shore.

"Why does Isaac deserve your forgiveness, your help," she sobbed, "while you continue to punish yourself?"

Steeling himself against the sound of her voice, the pleading, the pain, he worked with James and the other crewmen to shove the large rowboat farther into the water. But when the time came to jump in, he returned to shore.

"David, you can't stay," James yelled, still standing by the boat, waist deep in water. "The fight is heading for the pier."

Already the shouting had grown closer. "Don't worry about me," David assured him. "I'm a pirate. I've lived through worse than this."

James hesitated as if he would argue further, then glanced amongst his crew, the two women, and an injured man. He shook his head, his features grim, and climbed into the longboat. "Row," he ordered his oarsmen.

David watched as they moved away, and his eyes connected with Amelia's. The sorrow he saw there matched his own. God, how he'd miss her. He should return to the doctor's house, retrieve his violin, and find someplace safe to go before the enraged slaves found him, but he couldn't break from her haunting stare.

She was right. He and Isaac were much the same, and yet, he would never begrudge Isaac's happiness. Although the reason stumped him. Was Isaac the better man? As the distance between him and Amelia grew, the question plagued him. He paced the sand even as the sounds of breaking glass and splintering wood reached his ears.

David's father had humiliated him for as long as he could remember with incessant rants about his shortcomings. His humiliation had continued even after he'd left. A prisoner of pirates, he'd been treated as less than a man, trapped on a ship, taking orders from whoever gave them. As a slave, his abasement had only become worse. A master had controlled his every action, allowing him no free will at all. Then to kill an innocent… Just like how Isaac had attempted to kill him. Still, he accepted Isaac's actions. He understood them. So, why couldn't he accept his own?

Life as a slave had required more strength and will than he'd thought he'd had. That kind of hardship did something to a man, made him unforgiving, ruthless. It hadn't been until Amelia walked into his life that any softer emotions had risen to the surface. Water splashed over his feet and calves as he stepped into the waves. He clenched and flexed his hands, the ache in his chest turning to full-out pain, as if some essential part of him had been ripped away.

What made one man worthy of love and happiness, and another doomed to a lonely existence? Isaac didn't question his good fortune—he took life as it came.

David waded deeper, drawn by the need to follow his

heart. Maybe it was time to stop drifting through life and, instead, take control of it. It had felt good to stand up for Isaac. Time to stand up for himself, and to do that he needed to face his father. He would judge himself, rather than let others decide his value, and he would take what life offered with no objections, no guilt. For himself, and for Amelia. No longer would he be a coward, afraid his father's opinions were true.

His pulse raced. The longboat was nearly to the ship. He stripped off his borrowed shirt, ready to swim as if the very devil were on his trail. One thought stopped him short. His violin. But he didn't have time to go back. If he did, the ship would sail off, taking Amelia with it. An image of his mother presenting the violin to him flashed through his mind before he dove into the ocean toward Amelia.

• • •

David. Amelia's stomach filled with giddy flutters. She stood, and her legs wobbled beneath her. "Stop rowing!" She pointed to David swimming toward them. "He's changed his mind."

"Sit down, Miss Archer, or you're sure to fall in." James tugged on her arm until she sat, but looked back and released a sigh. "Turn her about," he ordered the oarsman. "Then make speed."

The longboat raced toward David. The shore behind him was riddled with escaped slaves ravaging everything they could, no doubt eager to destroy the place that had treated them so poorly. Her spirits dimmed. Were they the reason David had jumped into the water? She wrung her hands, the wait unbearable. The boat reached him in a matter of moments, and she held her breath as they hoisted him aboard and resumed their prior course.

James slapped David on the back. "I'm glad you came to your senses."

With a nod, David sat on the seat next to her and gasped for air.

"Your wound." She peered at the stitches in his side, his bandage gone. No blood. At least that was a blessing. She reached out, but stopped short of touching the battered skin. "Is it—"

"I'm fine." David took her hand and brought it to his chest. "More than fine actually, now that I'm with you."

He looked at her with contentment and warmth, a smile on his lips, even as he panted for air. Had she ever seen him so happy? Still, what he'd said on the beach… "What made you change your mind?"

"As I stood in the sand and watched this boat carry you away from me, I realized that nothing matters more to me than you." He brushed his hand along her cheek in a gentle touch that brought tears to her eyes. "I love you."

Those three words stole her breath and infused her entire being with a sense of exhilaration so strong she felt faint. "But I thought…"

"All I know is that you make me want to be a better man. Hell, I *am* a better man when I'm with you. And if you'll have me, I'll be the best husband you could ever want. Marry me, Amelia."

"Marry you?" The shock gave her heart pause. "I haven't changed my mind. I want to travel to my family in England."

He didn't so much as blink. "I know. We'll go together."

"You'd do that for me?"

"I'll do it for the both of us." He clasped her hand harder to his chest, a flicker of worry in his eyes. "Marry me. Please."

"Yes." The answer came out in a shaky whisper as emotion clogged her throat. He loved her.

David lowered his head and brushed his lips over hers in a thorough yet tender kiss. "I promise I'll make you happy."

She wrapped her arms around his neck and kissed him back, her heart filled to overflowing. "You already do."

The longboat pulled up alongside the ship and, one by one, the passengers climbed to the deck. David rose to his feet. They'd board this ship with even less than what they'd taken when they'd been cast off the last. Even his shirt was gone…and his violin.

"Your violin." He'd left it behind.

"I didn't have time to get it."

She glanced toward shore. *Was there a way*?

He took her hand in his, bringing her attention to him, still dripping from his swim. "No worries. There will be other violins, but there will never be another you." He pulled her to her feet and guided her to the ladder. "Come, Beauty. Let's go back to England."

To England, and her family. A true sense of happiness bloomed in her chest. David had opened her eyes to a new world, one filled with promise and love. He'd taught her what was real and what was not. He'd saved her life in more ways than one, and now this wonderful man was hers. She was a lucky woman indeed.

Epilogue

David stared down at his borrowed suit. It had been quite some time since he'd worn fine garments such as these. They felt foreign and uncomfortable. He closed his eyes and took a deep breath before knocking on his father's front door. He would have let more time pass before this visit. After all, they'd arrived at port just short of an hour ago. But James had been tenacious. He wanted to know David had been reunited with their father before he set sail again. In a fortnight, James, Charity, and his crew would be off to Africa at Isaac's request. Isaac, Ruth, and their young babe would return to his people there.

Amelia's gloved hand wrapped around his. "He's going to be relieved to see you."

David forced a smile. "I'm sure you're right." His father would be relieved, at first.

The door swung open, and an elderly man with stark white hair and a large nose stood before them. He looked the same as he always had—impassive and dignified, even when he would slip candy into David's pocket.

"Hello, Godfrey," David greeted the butler.

Godfrey's eyes widened for the briefest instant before he recovered to his usual stoic state. "Mr. David." That deep voice wobbled a bit, but he maintained his composure. "Mr. Lamont will be eager to see you. Please follow me." He inclined his head toward Amelia. "Miss."

They walked down the main corridor of the stately residence he'd once called home, the familiar scent of furniture polish permeating the air. David knew full well where they were going. His father rarely left his study. He'd always cared more for work than anything else.

The closer they came to his father, the tighter David's stomach clenched. He hadn't seen Gordon Lamont in more than a year, and that last meeting had been filled with shouting and spite. David ground his teeth in anticipation, and when they reached the doorway, he stepped forward. "Allow me."

He lifted his chin and entered the study. "Father," he said to the man sitting behind the large mahogany desk.

His father's head snapped up. "David?" He rose and crossed to the door, a bewildered look on his face. Strong and sturdy, his father had been barely touched by age, save his graying hair. They stood eye to eye for a full minute, his father's gaze traveling over David as if he couldn't believe what he was seeing, before he pulled him into a hug that squeezed the air from David's lungs.

David stiffened. His father hadn't shown him affection in years. But once the initial shock wore off, he relaxed and hugged him back. The moment would be fleeting, he was sure. Best enjoy it while he could.

"It's damned good to see you," his father rasped before he released David and studied him once more, grabbing his shoulder and giving it a shake. He glanced toward the door and spotted Amelia. "And who do you have with you?"

Amelia stepped forward and settled a hand on David's arm, offering him strength. Although he'd been determined to come here alone, now he thanked the heavens she'd insisted she join him.

He settled his hand over hers. "Father, allow me to introduce my future wife, Miss Amelia Archer."

His father nodded, a broad grin on his face. "Welcome, Miss Archer." He turned toward the decanters on a table by the window behind his desk. "This calls for a drink. Join me?" In short order, he returned with two glasses of liquor and a goblet of sherry, handing them out with glee. "What happened to you? Where have you been?"

He'd rather not discuss all that had happened, not with his father, who would judge him for his every action. "Doesn't matter. It's over now, and I'm putting it behind me." He'd come here to inform the man that he would live his life as he saw fit, no matter what his father wanted. A thousand times, he'd rehearsed in his head what he'd say and now he couldn't remember a thing.

His father hesitated as if tempted to push for answers, then acquiesced. "I'm so glad you're back." His father took a long drink from his glass. "You should have never gone on that ship. You belong on land…here."

David nearly growled his frustration. And so it would begin already, not five minutes after their reunion. "I won't work in your business." He didn't desire to, and he never would.

As expected, his father's brows slanted in displeasure. "Will you marry and raise a family without money?"

David suppressed a sigh. "Don't worry. I wouldn't dream of asking you for money." He thought he'd feel more anger, more outrage and contempt, but none of those emotions rose to the surface. Although physically his father appeared strong and hale, he had a vulnerability about him David had never detected before, as if his will had weakened. David's voice softened. He had no urge to hurt his father, only to make him understand. "We've fought for years about what you want from me, and I've grown weary of it. My future will be mine to determine, with or without your approval." He peered at Amelia, a promise in his eyes. "Trust me, I will support my family either through music or another profession, but I will do it on my terms." Her responding smile made him feel like the luckiest man in the world.

His father shook his head. "Musicians are paid a pittance. You won't be able to live on those wages, and what other profession are you suited for?" Although his father's words held venom, he said them with less vehemence than expected. Perhaps it was true that absence made the heart grow fonder. "A man must support his family. A man must—"

"We'll be visiting my father soon," Amelia supplied. "He's a devoted patron of the arts. Maybe he can help David."

His father mumbled a curse. "David, you're like your mother—with your head in the clouds." He returned to the desk and sank into his chair. "It's because of your mother that I've pushed you so hard. You meant the world to her." He set aside his drink and raked a hand through his hair, tousling the usually tidy strands. "The two of you had a relationship I could never be a part of, only envy, and now

I'm failing her."

"You're not failing her," David said. "She's the one who introduced me to music. She told me I could do anything I wanted to with my life."

"And she was right," his father muttered. His eyes met David's. "How about a compromise? I offer you patronage for your music for three years, and if after that time, you can't make a decent living in that manner, you are welcome to come work for me to supplement that income, if you want to."

What? "I don't understand. Why would you make such an offer, after all this time?"

His father's chin quivered. "I thought you were dead… and it made me come to understand what a fool I've been, demanding you do as I say, regardless of what you wanted… I can't lose you again."

David's first instinct was to question his father's sincerity, but the sorrow in his father's eyes, the regret… The resentment he'd held for so very long faded like a wisp of smoke. He approached the desk and rested a hand on his father's shoulder. "You won't lose me ever again. And I accept your offer. Thank you."

His father nodded but avoided his gaze. He'd never been comfortable showing emotion. Still, he clasped David's hand and held it tight.

David cleared his throat and set his glass on the desk. "Now, I suppose I should go see my sisters, or they'll have a fit that I waited so long to seek out their company. Would you like to come with us?"

"I would." His father rose from his seat, and David glimpsed the tears in his eyes. "I'll have the carriage sent around," he said as he left the room.

David exhaled a long breath and returned to Amelia's side.

Her face glowed with a bright smile. "That went better than I could have hoped."

Very true. He returned her smile, his heart lighter than it had ever been before. "I'm not the same man who stood before him last, and apparently he's changed, too." He set her goblet on the desk and took both of her hands in his. "Are you sure you're ready to become a musician's wife?" Even with his father's help, it wouldn't be easy for her. He wouldn't blame her if she changed her mind.

Amelia's eyes sparkled with warmth and love. "I don't care what you choose to do for a living as long as we're together."

Such an amazing woman. "You've always accepted me for who I am."

"And I always will."

For the longest time, he'd hidden in the shadows as bitterness ate him up inside, destroying him bit by bit. Then along came an angel on a sinking ship. Only through her love and guidance had he seen the light and stepped out of the shadows to become the man he was destined to be. His angel, his beauty. He'd love her for now and for always.

Author's Note

Now that I look back, it's crazy, but initially I had planned to have James, the hero of the first book in the Love on the High Seas trilogy *Tempting the Pirate*, discover that David had died. Poor David.

My critique partner Barbara Longley was the one to suggest that David survive and have a book of his own. She's such a wise woman. Then came the hard part... What the heck happened to David? We knew that he'd been kidnapped by the crew of *Neptune's Mercy* and later escaped in Madagascar. *Hmm*. What then?

I researched Madagascar in the 1700s and found very little, sad to say. But I did come across an interesting book, *Robert Drury's Journal*. Over the years, there's been some dispute over whether this story is true or not. Some say it was actually written by Daniel Defoe as a piece of fiction. Regardless, the book tells the story of how Robert Drury became a slave to a Madagascar prince and later escaped. Whether the tale is real or fictional, the descriptions of Madagascar are believed to be true. With that knowledge, I read the book to get a background of what David might have gone through as a slave in that region. Really interesting stuff.

From there, because *Beauty's Curse* is the second book in a pirate trilogy, I needed a pirate, so I decided that David had joined up with a pirate ship after he escaped. His internal demons were already well established. His whole reason for sailing in the first place was because of his father's scorn.

I had my hero, a tortured soul, who sailed the seas to escape life, but I needed a heroine to wake him up and make him realize what he's missing. I've always been fascinated by the concept of luck and all the superstitions that surround it. And pirates were extremely superstitious people. Who could blame them? Their lives were always at risk, because of the weather, the battles they fought, and the need to avoid those who would bring them to justice.

So why not place an unlucky heroine on a pirate ship and see what happens? *Beauty's Curse* was a lot of fun to write. I always learn so much with each story, and this time I got to research pirate superstitions. First, women aboard ship were considered bad luck. Amelia had the odds stacked against her even before she stepped on deck. Then there were some really strange ones: whistling, sneezing to the left while boarding with your left foot first, and sailing on Thursdays or Fridays. All were no good. And forget about having bananas on board. Ha! Needless to say, it wasn't all that difficult to establish the pirate crew's growing wariness toward Amelia. And once that was present, the rest of the story just poured out.

Amelia and David were such a well-matched couple. I

hope you enjoyed spending time with them as much as I did. My next book in the series involves a female pirate. So cool! She must steal a priceless artifact from the hero. Hee hee. I love the whole conflict in this one. Stay tuned.

Acknowledgments

Thank you to Jeff, Brenna, and Megan for your steadfast support and love. You make my days a joy. To Ron and Shirley Bores, thank you for all you've done for me on this crazy ride. From your constant encouragement to distributing my books to all the folks in the Stratford area, you've gone above and beyond.

Huge thanks to my editor Erin Molta, whose advice is always right on the mark. And of course, to my critique partners and friends Barbara Longley and Wyndemere Coffey, who pore over my books and help guide me in the right direction. I don't know what I'd do without you.

A happy wave to the Midwest Fiction Writers, a family of Minnesota romance writers who are always there for me, whether my news is good or bad. And thank you to the Romance Writers of America, an amazing organization that helps writers reach for success.

Last, but certainly not least, thank you to my readers. Your awesome messages and reviews make this all worthwhile. If you'd like to chat, feel free to visit with me on Twitter or Facebook.

I hope you enjoyed David and Amelia's story. Next up is the fight for the Ruby Cross. Catherine, a female pirate, needs it to save her son, but first she must steal the priceless artifact from Captain Thomas Glanville, a man not so easily crossed.

About the Author

A small town girl with a big imagination, Tamara Hughes had no idea what to do with her life. After graduating from college, she moved to a big city, started a family and a job, and still struggled to find that creative outlet she craved. An avid reader of romance, she gave writing a try and became hooked on the power of exploring characters, envisioning adventures, and creating worlds. She enjoys stories with interesting twists and heroines who have the grit to surmount any obstacle, all without losing the ability to laugh. To learn more, stop by her website: www.tamarahughes.com